IN BLOOD AND STONE

To Paolina —
Enjoy !

IN BLOOD AND STONE

A ZOEY STONE MYSTERY

Florence Noonan

Florence Noonan

www.florencenoonan.com

ISBN: 1515091511
ISBN 13: 9781515091516
Library of Congress Control Number: 2015911372
CreateSpace Independent Publishing Platform
North Charleston, South Carolina
Published in the United States of America
www.florencenoonan.com

With love to:
Stephen and Annie Kirby,
Matthew and Nathaniel

ACKNOWLEDGEMENTS

I cannot thank Judith Campbell enough for her support and encouragement. As a mystery writer, she gave me lots of suggestions, and invited me into her writers' group. As a UU minister, her mission has been to open doors for others. She certainly did that for me.

My editor, Jennifer Caven belongs in an Editors' Hall of Fame. She is phenomenal. Her knowledge of writing, her critical eye and her willingness to help sharpen the skills of this writer helped shape this debut novel. Thank you for your generosity.

Thanks to Hank Phillippi Ryan who gave me advice and encouragement.

A special thanks to my first readers, Charlene Bailey and Barbara Feeley whose comments not only encouraged me, but pointed out areas that needed attention. Thanks for sticking with me from the beginning. It has been terrific working with the two of you.

Thanks to the 3-on-3 writing group for all your suggestions: Ruth Blake, Judy Campbell, Pam Claughton, Vaughn Keller, Robert Knox, Dolores Ricco and Charlotte Simpson.

Thanks also to other readers who helped with portions of the book: Diana Lee, Una McMahon, Sandra Michellotti, Pam Pierson, Kathy Rossow and Dianne Yelverton.

Thanks to David Khoshtinat for helping me come up with the perfect title.

For support and encouragement, a special thanks to Dennis Cozzens, John Goodson, Sandy Mansfield and William Minichiello. The world would be a far better place if it were populated with more folks like you.

IN BLOOD AND STONE

CHAPTER 1

"Let's cut to the chase. You're on administrative leave. Unpaid."

Zoey Stone swallowed. She had not expected this. "For how long?"

Principal Peter Kroger, bald and squat with grey eyes, wore a navy blue suit, white shirt and blue striped tie. He placed his hands on his desk and leaned forward. "Indefinite."

Anxiety pricked her stomach, but she controlled herself and calmly matched his stare, hoping she appeared confident. "Peter, I understand I made a serious mistake, but—"

"Serious isn't the word." Kroger stood straight up. "Catastrophic is more like it. I thought you should be fired, but the School Board, well, for some reason, they wanted to keep you."

"I realize that the attendance roster—"

"I know the circumstances, Zoey." He continued to glare at her, and a corner of his mouth turned up. "You marked him present and he wasn't. According to you, he was here in school at the same time that he was robbing a citizen at an ATM. At gunpoint. You do know attendance is a legal document, don't you?"

Zoey nodded once.

"His defense lawyer loved your mistake." Kroger threw his arms up in the air. "Made his case for reasonable doubt."

She glanced at the floor and shifted her weight in the chair which made it squeak. She felt as exposed as a fish tossed up on a riverbank, frantic for oxygen. "If you remember, I corrected my mistake as soon as I caught it."

"Not good enough. His attorney made it look like you tried to cover up." He settled back into his chair. "It was pure luck that his family moved away." He rubbed his palm over his face.

She knew he disliked her, wanted to get rid of her, although she wasn't sure why. "My point is, when other teachers have made mistakes, well, they have been treated more leniently."

Kroger triangled his fingers, then his mouth curled into a smirk. "Have they now?"

"Yes. With all due respect, I don't understand the severity of this, well… this punishment."

He tapped his fingers together. "To be honest, I don't understand what Principal Caputo saw in you."

Zoey sat bolt upright. "That's rather harsh."

"'Cares for these kids like they are her own.' That's what he said about you. 'Passion for justice. Makes intuitive leaps.'" He continued to tap his fingers. "'Analytical.'"

"I like to think that about myself."

He dismissed her response with a vague wave of his hand. "Frankly, in the year that I've been here, I haven't seen it."

She felt her shoulders start to slump, but she caught herself and squared them.

He leaned back in his chair and studied her, then grinned, a Cheshire Cat kind of grin. "Perhaps I am being too harsh. I understand why Paul Caputo hired you to teach these kids. You had the right credentials, Master's Degree in psychology, special education certification. He said you helped build the program. It's to your credit. Most charter schools don't teach at-risk students." He wiped his mouth with the back of his hand. "But I'm concerned about you."

Bullshit, Zoey thought. He was building a case to dismiss her, and she knew it. "I appreciate it. The concern I mean. But I'm fine."

The Annie Sullivan Charter School ran in her veins, as crucial to her as her blood. "Of course I was disappointed when Paul Caputo retired." She felt a catch in her throat. What a team they had been for ten years. Great results with tough kids. But just now, she needed to deal with this jerk who called himself a principal. "Your last evaluation of my work was positive."

"Lukewarm, at best, I'd say."

"Well, you have to admit—"

"Nothing. I have to admit nothing." He stood and took a deep breath which puffed out his chest. "Now, I have to bring your substitute up to speed. He stood and reached out his hand. "Your plan book?"

For a moment, she thought about refusing. However, she thought it best to cooperate, or at least appear to do so. She dug her binder from her tote bag and slid it onto his desk. Her lessons, each one thought out and reworked, again and again, evolving, ever-changing to meet her students' needs. Her sweat. Her soul.

"Your administrative leave starts now. Call it a sabbatical if you want."

Thinking she was expected to help her substitute with the briefing, she remained seated where she was.

Kroger cleared his throat. "In private." He extended his arm toward the door.

When Zoey left his office, she shut the door ever so softly.

CHAPTER 2

Three days after Zoey Stone's rough dismissal from the principal's office, a storm—sudden and unexpected—assaulted Plymouth, Massachusetts. Lightning bleached the late morning clouds outside the windows in her apartment at 22 Brewster Street.

The necklace she was creating was nearly finished. Just as she aimed a wire at a hole drilled through the guts of a bead, thunder walloped the sky and reverberations shook her window pane like a demented snare drum. Startled, she whipped the wire in the air, sending the beads sliding off, one by one. She lunged to catch them, but they clinked between the slats in the grates that lead to her heating system, then disappeared.

She felt a heaviness in her chest as she realized they were irretrievable. Drawing in a breath, she walked to a window in her third floor apartment that looked over the roof of the Governor Bradford Inn.

Rain meandered down the glass, distorting her image. Barely five feet tall with a small frame, large hazel eyes and freckles across her nose, she looked more like one of her students, appearing much younger than her thirty-two years. Several years ago, she'd had a butterfly tattooed on her wrist, which just added to her youthful appearance. When teaching, she covered her face with foundation to hide her freckles, but otherwise wore no makeup. Usually she pulled her auburn hair back from her face and attempted to tame it with a headband. No matter how many different shampoos or lotions she tried, nothing corralled the curls that frizzed in all directions.

She leaned her forehead against the cool glass and sighed. It wasn't so much about the beads, nor was it about her meeting with the principal, as difficult as that had been.

Perhaps it was that advertisement her older sister, Monica Stone-Lewis, had brought with her in a dawn visit that morning. After Monica left, Zoey had shoved the nagging information from her mind and, unable to sleep, had worked on her necklace.

Now those misgivings were surfacing like pond scum. She could no longer deny the horrible possibilities behind her sister's investigative reporting. Although Monica was prone to exaggeration, her basic facts were usually right. With her husband Kurt, Monica produced a monthly online magazine, *Front and Center*, with the help of freelance journalists. Zoey reached into the wastebasket, picked out the two yellow papers she had balled up that morning and spread them out on the table. Inhaling deeply, she knew she needed to sort out her feelings of exasperation with her sister from the implications of those pages.

The brrrrng of the doorbell had awakened Zoey that morning. She had slumber-walked down two flights of stairs and flicked on the outside light. She'd paused before opening the door and glanced through the window. Monica was pacing back and forth on the porch. Zoey shook her head as she unlocked the door. Fashion boots and a sequined sweater were a bit much before breakfast; but then Monica was always a bit much.

The autumn air chilled Zoey when she stepped outside. "'Bout time you answered the door," Monica said. The distant eeeoooeeeooo of a siren seemed to emphasize her urgency, as did the crimson haze on the early morning horizon. Her sister waved the yellow papers in front of her. "This is despicable."

"Despicable. Yes. Dawn has barely cracked."

Monica brushed by her and entered the foyer. "Dawn—whether cracked or not—isn't relevant." She thrust the papers at her. "Something has to be done about this. And immediately."

Zoey held up her hands, refusing to take the sheets. "Not before coffee. Coffee. Now that's what I call relevant." She knew her sister wouldn't leave until she'd expounded on whatever it was in those damn papers. She plodded back up the stairs with Monica yapping behind her. "Sabbatical," Zoey called over her shoulder. "Does that word mean anything to you? To me, for one, it means I can sleep late."

"Phooey. Who takes a sabbatical in October? When are you going to admit what's really going on?"

5

"Just because you think something demands immediate attention, that doesn't give you the right to barge in at this ungodly hour. Who appointed you 'Goddess of the Important?'" She clumped up the stairs and entered her kitchen.

"Don't be such a wimp."

As Zoey made coffee, she kept her back to her sister and listened to the clack-clack of high-heeled boots on hardwood floor. Who does she think she is? Zoey thought. Queen Monica. Probably some nonsense in those papers. Father spoiled her rotten. She shifted her weight from one foot to the other, feeling the familiar tug again—the desire to have what Monica had shared with him. Wanting him to love her like he had loved her sister. Sometimes she felt her relationship with her father had been like a desert, barren and shifting. Now, her memories of him were as elusive as grains of sand slipping through her fingers.

Inhaling the aroma, she was grateful for the time the brewing took, so she could calm down. She clinked mugs on the table, poured coffee, then sat, and her sister joined her.

"Dangerous stuff," Monica said, sliding the papers across the table. "I will expose this website."

At first glance, the internet advertisement appeared harmless enough. OmniGenetics.com promised parents of a baby up to the age of one the option of choosing traits for their child. The list included:

- immunity from disease
- superior intelligence
- athletic ability
- attractive features
- height
- longevity

She looked up. "This seems ludicrous. A one-year-old child can't be altered like this."

Monica nodded. "I agree. From my research, any genetic modification would have to be injected directly into the embryo. And even that is not possible yet."

"But who would buy this?" Zoey asked. "Certainly not educated people. They would know better." She frowned and was silent, tapping her finger against her mouth. "Ignorant people might be hooked by the ad, but they would still have questions. It does concern their children, after all."

"Oh, don't be so damn naïve." Monica banged her cup on the table. "Not all parents are so careful. What about those idiots putting their two-year-olds in beauty pageants? All for the glory of Mom. They'd jump on that trait for 'attractive features.'"

"You may have a point."

The words EXAMPLES of DONORS were centered on the page. Six square photos were lined up underneath, a child's smiling face in each one. The caption for each stated one of the six traits. Three boys. Three girls.

Zoey shuddered. If Monica was right… Would these creeps actually take blood from kids? Were their parents paid for their children's blood like some unholy sacrifice? "This is all so bizarre."

"Keep reading."

The parents were instructed to send for a free kit that included a booklet explaining the process, the materials to collect saliva from their child, and a package to mail the sample back to the lab. The cost for shipping the kit was $2.95.

The ad continued. For $2000, the child's DNA would be modified with the gene for the chosen trait. That reconstructed DNA would be placed in a 'medium' that could be injected.

Although Zoey had her own thoughts, she asked, "What do you think of all this?"

"It's scary. These criminals have no scruples. What 'medium' would be used? Something cheap and readily available. Certainly nothing safe or sterile, that would cost too much money. So exactly what would be injected? They could use dog pee as donor material for all the consumer knows."

"How much harm could be done?" Zoey felt anger stir her blood. How could anyone risk hurting a child?

"Precisely, my question."

"I hear what you're saying, Monica. Still, I do think parents would be skeptical."

"People believe what they want to believe. The price is low so people will buy the service. That's what I think. Worldwide, these monsters will make a fortune." Monica snickered. "I've already sent for the kit. The customer can't download the booklet. They send everything snail mail. Can you believe it?"

"Maybe they only expect money from the shipping price on the kit. How many hits on the site?"

"Close to a million in a few days."

Zoey whistled.

"So you see the urgency."

"Say they leave the site up for two weeks. They get half a million orders for kits at two-ninety-five a whack. If a kit even exists. That's a lot of money. They take the orders. Then shut down the site. No kits are mailed because they don't exist. Maybe that's why the snail mail. People won't expect anything for a few days. When the customers complain, the thieves stall. Apologize and say they will mail out another kit. Take the money and run. It would be hard to find them."

"No. No. You don't get it." Monica pushed her blonde hair back from her face with both hands and leaned her elbows on the table. "Those assholes want the suckers to buy the whole package. They'll want the two thousand dollars."

"Pretty risky to leave the site up too long."

Monica's eyes flashed, then went hard. "They want the big bucks. Like I said. They'd take the risk. Any idiot can see that."

Zoey stood. "Yeah, you're always right. God forbid someone challenges you."

"It's real simple. All you have to do is explain it to David, he'll bring it to that detective friend of his," Monica said. "What's his name?"

"Tom Madsen." Zoey picked up the mugs and placed them in the sink. She faced her sister and leaned against the counter. For a moment she thought about David Roth, a guidance counselor at the Annie Sullivan Charter School. A man she had shared her life with for the past ten years. "I ended it with him a month ago."

Monica stared at her, her mouth open. "I'm sorry. I thought you two were a sure thing." She stood and fidgeted with the cuff on her sweater. "I'll touch base with you later," she said, waved awkwardly and left the apartment.

Wind rattled the window and refocused Zoey on her view of the harbor. After walking to the kitchen, she made toast and spread on strawberry jam. At that moment, her cell phone rang. "Hello." Then she answered her brother-in-law's question. "No, what's up?" As she listened, her eyes grew wide and she fumbled the toast, almost dropping her breakfast on the floor. "What! He's gone missing!"

CHAPTER 3

Jackie Ravinski, twenty-six and a graduate of the Annie Sullivan Charter School, was awakened by the howling of a siren which faded as the vehicle rushed by her apartment. The sunrise cast a soft crimson backlight on her blinds. She yawned and turned on her side in the futon. Although her hips were wide, out of proportion to an otherwise slender body, they added to her attractiveness, as did her long copper-colored hair. Her brown eyes were cautious. She snuggled back into her blanket. No need to be responsible, she thought, not at this moment anyhow.

She wanted to be the best mom ever to her six-year-old son, Will, but that was also her torment. How could she know if she were doing a good job when her own childhood had been such a mess?

Her thoughts drifted back to yesterday. It had been a good day and she smiled, remembering the ferry ride, Will's first, to Martha's Vineyard. Sun had sparkled like sugar on the clear blue water. Standing on tiptoes, gripping the railing, Will had enjoyed the wind on his face as it tousled his wavy blonde hair. He was wearing a Red Sox sweatshirt and black sweat pants. Although thin like his mother, Will had surprised his T-Ball coach by whacking the ball into the outfield.

When he finally sat down next to Jackie on the boat, he was fingering a bracelet made of blocks etched with letters that spelled out his name. Between the blocks, tiny bloodstones were attached. When Zoey Stone had given him the gift, she had told him that the stones were amulets that protected the person wearing them from evil.

A few seats in front of them, a young girl sat next to a man who was reading a book. Beside his feet, a golden retriever was stretched out with its head on its paws flicking its tail every now and then.

After a while, Will had pulled a puzzle book from his backpack. "Can you do a really hard maze?" he asked his mother, and then turned to a page.

"I've never tried a really hard one." She dug a pen out of her purse and traced a route that zig-zagged into a dead end. "Argh!"

Will had laughed. "You can go back to the beginning."

"No way." Jackie continued to find her way through the maze until she hit another blocked path. "This is hard."

"There are easier ones, Mom."

She had flipped through the book. "Here's a picture to color." Will climbed into her lap and leaned against her. "I like the one of the wolves best."

"Why?"

"They're way better than lions."

Then he had hopped down, dug a small red ball from his pocket and bounced it on the floor close to the dog. The animal had lifted its head and sniffed the air.

"That's gonna get old, real quick."

He had bounced the ball again, but this time, the retriever ignored it and laid its head back on its paws.

"If it happens again we'll have to put the ball away."

"I was just trying to see if the dog would go after it."

"It's not okay." Jackie had pulled an Etch-a-Sketch from his backpack. "Would you like to do this?"

He had slouched in the seat, turning the ball over and over in his hands. She frowned for a minute and then started to sketch a pattern. "Look at all the cool shapes I can make, dude." Will scrambled back into her lap, and they drew pictures together.

When he had tired of that, he asked, "Can I get a snack, Mom?"

"Yes."

"Do I have to use my own money?"

"No."

"M&Ms?"

"No candy."

"Gummy Bears?"

"Gummy Bears are candy. Let's see what they have." Jackie had taken her son's hand and they had walked past the dog and the girl, whose head was resting against the shoulder of the man. Then, swaying gently with the motion of the ferry, Jackie and Will had climbed the stairs to the top deck where the snack bar was located.

Still smiling, she pulled the blanket up to her chin, rolled over on the futon and went back to sleep. She was unaware that Will was nowhere in the apartment.

CHAPTER 4

"You'll get 'lectrocuted. Turn that damn TV off 'til that storm passes."

Guy Falcone ignored his mother's warning coming from that shit-can of a kitchen. Grabbing the remote, he blared the volume on the flat screen as Arnold Schwarzenegger crashed through the jungle in a re-run of *Predator*. Guy drew hard on his cigarette and blew smoke from the corner of his mouth.

Buff and proud of his tattoos, he slouched in an armchair where the ash had spilled from a saucer onto the fabric. But no matter, the navy material was faded and torn. He wore a tank top and jeans. His boots were slung up on the Salvation Army coffee table where a bottle of Budweiser was leaving circles on the surface. A stench filled Madeline Falcone's house, probably mold in the basement, but what could he do with no fucking money? Just out of prison after four crap-ass years. His mother's dump would have to do 'til he could figure something out.

Lightning flashed outside, sending Schwarzenegger's face into electronic spasms.

A week ago, clouds had threatened rain as he had slumped down to hide in the driver's seat of his mother's car which Jackie Ravinski would not have recognized. After turning off the engine because of its rattling and clunking, he had spied on her apartment on School Street until she had come out wearing jeans and a sweatshirt. Still one hot babe. But goddamn her. Not visiting him in that hellhole after the first year. Not a word from her. Abandoning him like that. How could he still love her? But he did.

When the apartment door slammed shut, Will had bounded down the steps, his blonde hair bouncing. Why the fuck hadn't she cut it? Looked like a freaking girl. She had him dressed in a hoodie and jeans with sneakers. When she hefted Will into the safety seat in her Chevy, he had felt an urge to help; she was such a little woman, but he had remained where he was—hidden.

He had followed her to Plymouth Beach. Not being spotted was difficult because the SUV's clanking was even worse when it was in gear. As soon as she parked, Will had jumped from the car and raced to the ocean, stopping where the water slapped the shore. When Jackie had caught up to him he was already chucking stones at the waves. Had a good arm, but then what else could Guy expect?

On the TV screen, Schwarzenegger was blasting a machine gun when Guy felt a whack on his chest right across his mermaid tattoo, right where the tail curled up.

"Get them dirty things off my table." His mother slapped a spatula on his boot, spraying bits of grease into the air.

He yanked his feet from the table. "What the fuck you doing, Ma?"

"Trying to straighten you up." Ash dangled from a cigarette in her mouth, as she slid a plate with an egg sandwich onto the table where the boots had been. "Here's breakfast."

In spite of his annoyance, Guy felt sorry for her. He knew he was a disappointment to her. Being an only child meant no siblings who might have made it. No one she could be proud of. At forty-nine, she already had a matronly figure, and her hair had turned completely gray, not one brown strand left. She kept it cropped short for convenience, and did nothing to conceal the dark circles that rimmed her eyes. Today she was wearing brown polyester slacks, a green T-shirt and a soiled apron. He hated her constant smoking, lighting one cigarette after another.

The egg smelled good. "You going to work today?" He took a bite of the sandwich.

"Working the supper shift tonight." She put the spatula on the coffee table.

"That cheap bastard keeps you part time so he doesn't have to pay you no benefits. He ever give you a raise? That nursing home must bring in a bundle for him." He laughed. "Sunny Days for him, for sure."

His mother wiped her hands on her apron. "I'm putting flowers on your father's grave. You should come."

Guy wiped his mouth with the back of his hand. "I never knew him."

"He was still your father. A good man. He couldn't help it if cancer took him when you were so young."

He took another bite of the sandwich. Appreciating the melted cheese, tomato and salad dressing on top of the egg, he had to give it to his mother. She could cook.

"And why aren't you out looking for work?"

"Won't do no good."

"Maybe Jake would take you on part time again at the garage, changing oil, fixing tires, like you did in high school."

Guy shrugged his shoulders. "I heard his business isn't doing so hot."

"That's an excuse. You go talk to him." He saw his mother's jaw muscles tighten.

"I already did."

"Don't you go getting involved with that Todd O'Malley again." She plopped into an armchair next to the couch. "He's the one got you into prison. Selling them drugs, like that."

"Todd didn't make me do nothing. I told you. I did it for Jackie and the baby." He swallowed the last of the beer. "Aren't you going overboard with stuff for Will?" He waved his hand toward a new Schwinn bike with training wheels tucked in a corner of the living room. Just the right size for a six year old. "And what's with the room upstairs? Painting it all blue. New bed, a closet full of clothes. Swing set outside. People will think he'll be living here."

"That Todd was responsible. You're a good boy."

"I ain't a boy. And where'd you get all the money for this stuff?"

"Never you mind. Will might be living with us. Never say no." Her eyes harbored hope.

"Ma, it really is too much stuff, and you can't afford it. If he does come over here, it'll be for short visits. Bring some of it back."

Thunder rumbled faintly somewhere in the east and lights flickered briefly in the room. She pushed herself out of the chair. "Where's that remote? Told you to turn it off." She picked it up from the coffee table and clicked the TV off.

He grimaced, and when she put the remote back down, he grabbed it and turned the television back on. "I'm no damn child."

"Then stop acting like one."

He stood, yanked on a leather jacket, punched his hand into his pocket and pulled out a set of keys.

"You aren't riding that bike in the rain." She stepped in front of him blocking his way. "Skid all over the place. Get yourself killed."

"I'll be okay."

"Take the SUV."

"Told you. I'll be okay." He gently squeezed her shoulders, moved her to one side and grabbed his helmet from the door knob. The front door slammed shut behind him just as Schwarzenegger blew a helicopter out of the sky.

He unlocked the chain securing his rundown Harley to the tree in front of the house. Although the storm had subsided, rain was still spitting. He stuffed the helmet on his head, mounted his cycle and revved it in place, feeling its power. His mood lightened as he kicked off and rode down Main Street, heading for the Union Fish Raw Bar and Restaurant.

CHAPTER 5

"Monica still there?" Zoey heard Kurt Lewis, her brother-in-law, ask. "No. What's up?" She pictured him: partially bald with a ring of hair around his head; bushy eyebrows; kind, steady, blue eyes; tall and thin.

"I'm not sure how to break this to you, so I'll just say it. Will is missing."

"What! How?"

"Came over the police scanner."

"Are you sure? That can't be real."

"Police went to Jackie's apartment a couple hours ago."

"But how could he be missing? Jackie must be out of her mind with worry—"

"Actually, she's a suspect."

"Suspect? That's crazy." She squeezed her eyes shut as if that darkness could block out the truth.

"Listen Zoey, it's nothing. They always look at family first."

"But I don't understand. She would have nothing to do with—"

"She's at the police station."

"Will, I can't believe it."

"Look, I've already alerted our subscribers by e-mail. Someone might know something about his disappearance. You never know. Anything that might help."

"Why on earth?" Her heart was beating faster than she thought was possible. "But Kurt, why would they go after Jackie?"

"Have the police ever been involved with her and Will for any reason? Maybe a nosy neighbor called the cops because she heard Jackie yelling at him? Or maybe the neighbor thought she saw abusive behavior?"

"Never."

"I would have thought they'd have gone after the ex-con father."

"Kurt, you do know he's in prison."

"Oh, you didn't know? Guy Falcone was released two weeks ago."

"What!"

"Figured you knew." Kurt sounded distracted. "Checking my notes. Ah, here it is. Detective Dahlbeck arrested Jackie Ravinski at her home at 7:15 this morning."

"Dahlbeck! That bastard!"

"Apparently, Falcone was a model prisoner."

"Dahlbeck can't punish Jackie's father, but he can get at her. He would want his revenge."

"What are you talking about?" Kurt asked.

"Jackie's father had an affair with Dahlbeck's wife. Used to visit her while Dahlbeck was on duty. Went on for a couple of years. They kept it a pretty good secret. But then, one day, the wife took off with Jackie's father and went to Vegas with him. She divorced Dahlbeck and got married in one of those little chapels."

"God damn!"

"So you see..."

"Wait. Hold on a second. I think I hear the door."

A clunk on the line. Thoughts spun in Zoey's head, and then muffled voices. Monica came on the phone. "Zoey, don't worry, it'll all work out."

"You don't know that. It can end horribly."

"Well, listen. We'll do what we can. Police will be doing what they usually do in these cases. Today, we'll investigate, you and me and Kurt. Whatever we think will be helpful. Then we'll put our heads together. Kurt will check with the police. Share what we've learned. Will's a super smart kid. It's not like he's totally helpless." Her voice cracked. "But, look. No matter what—we have to eat. I'll pick up takeout for tonight. Come around five, no...wait, make it six."

For a fleeting moment, some part in Zoey realized Monica's defenses were down, not for long, but they were down. This was the sister she loved so dearly.

"Jackie must be frantic!" Zoey said.

"Course she is."

"That Dahlbeck is a bastard."

"Zoey, are you listening to me?"

"Yes, yes, I'm listening."

"I mean about tonight. Did you hear me?"

"Five o'clock at your place."

"*S-I-X.* Make it six."

"Okay. Okay. Six."

There was a long pause. "Are you okay?"

"How could I be? Listen, Monica, I've got to get to the police station. See you tonight." As soon as she hung up, Zoey dug her keys out, hurried to her Jeep Wrangler and drove to Water Street where traffic was bumper to bumper. Although it was October, the day was warm and tourists were ambling across the street toward the waterfront, enjoying the day. Such a contrast to the urgency she felt. She forced her Jeep in front of a truck whose driver waved a fist and honked, but she didn't care and squeezed into line anyway, slowly creeping past Plymouth Rock. What must Jackie be feeling?

When she had parked at the police station and walked into the lobby, she was surprised to see David Roth talking to his childhood friend, Detective Tom Madsen. The two men had grown up together in the same neighborhood and had known each other since third grade. What was David doing there? Today was Sunday, so school wasn't in session. Knowing David as well as she did, if he had heard about Will, he would want to do whatever he could to help. It made sense. What better way to figure out how to help than by talking to his friend?

Desire for David stirred in her and mixed with the fear she felt for Will. That bothered her. She certainly didn't need confusion, not today. When he spotted her, he hurried over, cupped her elbow with his hand and then directed her to a corner of the lobby. "What are you doing here?"

"I was going to ask you the same thing. Is Jackie Ravinski here?"

"Zoey, there's nothing you can do."

"She's done nothing wrong."

"That may be true."

She crossed her arms. "*May* be?"

David rubbed the back of his neck. "Let the process run its course."

"But she's innocent."

"Then that will come out."

"How can you be so sure? Do you really trust the system that much?" Zoey's eyes filled with tears.

"I know Jackie's a good mother, and a lot is being done to find Will. Tom was telling me that cops from towns around Plymouth are out looking for him. Going door to door. Scouring empty fields—everywhere. Helicopters are already up. Volunteers are being organized for searches. I figure I can help out with that."

She looked at him as tears ran down her face. "An Amber Alert?" She couldn't think of anything else to ask and she felt foolish that she couldn't. "Did they do an Amber Alert for Will?"

"Wouldn't do any good. There's no description of a car. No way the public could help with that. Hell, Jackie couldn't remember if he was wearing pajamas or a T-shirt and shorts when he went to bed."

"What's happening to her now?"

"She's being questioned."

"Who?"

"Doesn't matter."

She hit him in his chest. "Tell me who, damnit!"

"Dahlbeck."

"Oh dear God!" She plopped into a chair. "I'm not going anywhere. I'll take Jackie home when he's done ripping her apart."

"It'll be a while." He stood there for a moment, as if unsure what to do. He walked back to Tom Madsen, said something, and both men looked over at her. Then they resumed their conversation and, occasionally, David glanced over at her.

She imagined her fingers tracing the outline of his face, massaging his temples when anxiety clouded his eyes, which it often did. She loved the way he tilted his head when he listened; the way he whistled while he cooked for her. Short for a man, he was just a few inches taller than she. His shoulders were broad, and because he worked out at the gym, his body was taut. Not exactly handsome, his looks were rugged, like Humphrey Bogart. Although she felt safe with him, she felt her vulnerability at the same time, which made her uncomfortable.

Sighing, she pulled her cell phone from her pocket and punched in a number. When voicemail answered, she left an urgent message. It was the least she could do for Jackie. How inadequate and helpless she felt!

A teenage girl with tattoos slouched in the lobby, reminding Zoey of Jackie when she was a troubled sixteen-year-old. David left Tom Madsen to deal with the teenager, crossed the lobby and sat next to Zoey.

"Wonder why they aren't talking to Guy; after all he's an ex-con."

"Tom said they tried this morning. His mother got hostile. Told them he wasn't there. Even with a Harley chained to a tree." David chuckled. "Imagine his mother driving a Harley. But they're going back with a warrant later."

"Can they get one?"

David shrugged. "Depends on the judge." In silence, they watched Tom Madsen write information on a clip board while the teenager shifted from one foot to another and back again. David asked, "Remember when Jackie was pregnant and thinking about dropping out of school?"

Zoey looked at him and half-smiled. "Yeah, I do. She was so confused. It was painful to watch."

"You got her through it."

"So did you. I remember her sobbing in your office. And not just once." She was quiet for a moment. "It wasn't just us. Having Will, well, that turned her around. She had to grow up in a hurry."

"True, but there you were, living with a colicky infant. Tutoring Jackie after teaching every day. The three of you in your tiny apartment." He shook his head. "I don't know how you did it."

"For sure, he wasn't an easy baby."

He placed his hand on her knee. "You made sure she graduated."

"Yes, but I wasn't in it alone. Lots of people pitched in. You went to the School Board with Paul Caputo and convinced them to help support her financially until she got into a welfare program."

"That was a tough sell. And he was one hell of a principal."

"I miss him."

"Me too."

"And you, bringing those meals over every other night."

"Guilty."

"I miss that too." Immediately, she wished she hadn't admitted to that.

"If you'd like," David said, "I can do it again."

She stared at the floor. "I'm sorry. Please don't."

He patted her knee. "That apartment of yours was so tiny. I could *not* stretch out my legs without banging my toes into a wall. "

"It wasn't that bad." Playfully, she punched him in the arm. Then she asked, "You know what I never got? Did you ever understand Jackie and Dara Lee being best friends?"

"Both came from lousy backgrounds. Connected that way, but they are very different people. Academically, Dara Lee did all right, but she never opened up to me. When she graduated, she was as sneaky and manipulative as the day she entered that school." He added, "I expect some day she'll get herself into serious trouble. And she won't be able to manipulate her way out."

The teenager left the police station; Tom Madsen walked over and stood in front of them with his legs slightly apart. "Zoey, good to see you." Tall and husky, his square face was strong and his blue eyes gentle. He had gained some weight since she'd last seen him, and his belly distended a bit over his belt.

Cocking his head toward the interior of the police station, he said to his friend, "Gotta go." David nodded.

CHAPTER 6

Guess she's had enough time to stew, Detective Dahlbeck thought while he watched Jackie Ravinski through the one-way mirror in the police station. A table and two empty chairs dominated the interview room. Leaning on the table, she sat in a metal chair, her face ashen and haunted.

He was damn good at interrogation and knew it, prided himself on it, actually. Enjoyed the game, being the cat, watching the mouse sweat, relishing the taste of fear. Believed himself to be a cop's cop. But this one would be especially sweet. That cock-sucker father of hers. He heard footsteps, and then a uniformed cop with sandy hair approached. "Ready, sir." Dahlbeck rubbed his nose, entered the room and sat facing her. The cop remained behind, watching through the one-way glass. Her breathing was shallow and quick which pleased Dahlbeck. He would break her down.

"What are you doing to find my son?"

He ignored her question. "How would you describe yourself as a mother?"

Her forehead wrinkled. "What's that got to do with anything? Will's out there—"

"Yes, yes," he interrupted. "There are no signs of anyone breaking into your apartment from outside. How can you explain that?"

The wrinkles grew deeper. "How would I know?" Her eyes darted back and forth. "My son. He's such a little boy. If—"

Again he cut her off. "Who else was with you last night?"

"No one. But what are you doing …"

"There was no struggle. Nothing was disturbed in Will's room. How can that be?"

"I need to get out of here. Find him." Her lip was trembling.

Piece of cake, he thought. "The bolt lock on the front door was too high for him to reach. Your pocketbook had your keys inside." He leaned in closer to her. "Where is he?" After waiting for a few moments, he added, "You didn't mean it. You snapped. A little boy like that can get on your nerves. It's understandable."

"You're wrong!" She glowered at Dahlbeck. "He's out there alone."

"Alone. I'm glad you admit that. A single mom. It must be difficult."

She shook her head, splayed her hands on her knees and stared at the floor.

Dahlbeck was annoyed. "You're young. A child can be a burden. Interfere with your own life. What you want to do." He watched her but she remained as she was. "You couldn't do it yourself so you asked Guy Falcone to help you."

Her head snapped up. "He's in prison."

"Released over two weeks ago. And you know it."

Her eyes grew wide.

What an actress, he thought. "Come now, Miss Ravinski. A man who sold drugs. A person like that can steal a child."

At that moment, the uniformed cop knocked on the door. "Detective, a word." Grumbling, Dahlbeck looked up. A stout man in a striped suit stepped into the room and handed him a card. "Jackson Addison. Zoey Stone hired me. Jackie Ravinski, you are my client. Do not say another word." His voice was firm. "Detective, if you are not going to charge her, you need to release her."

CHAPTER 7

Having returned from the kitchen, Monica examined a bowl of strawberries, chose one and popped it into her mouth. She was standing in the doorway of the office she shared with her husband when she overheard the end of his conversation with a fellow editor. "Did he give you any other ideas about searching for Will?"

Kurt turned in his chair. "Oh, didn't hear you come back." He rubbed his hand over his chin. "Not really. Cops are on the ball, doing what needs to be done."

When she moved to his side, she kissed him and offered him the fruit. Instead, he took her hand and brushed his lips against her fingertips.

"How do you think Zoey took the news about Will and Jackie?"

"Like you'd expect."

"Sometimes I wish we were closer. After all, we are sisters, but she puts up such walls."

"She the only one with bricks and mortar?"

Monica wrinkled her nose at her husband and pulled her hand away. She glanced at his computer screen. "'Missing and Exploited Children.' Anything helpful?"

"His name and photo are already registered. Fast work on someone's part."

"Well, that's something, anyway." She bit into another strawberry and peered at the screen again. "I see they mention Code Adam. Do you think it really helps when a store blasts out 'Code Adam, Code Adam' over the intercom?"

"Better than not doing it. If a missing child is spotted early enough, it could prevent a kidnapping. Depends how fast all the doors can be locked. Depends how fast the employees can make it to the exits."

"I suppose."

"Say, what do you think we're missing in all the things everyone is doing to find him?"

She plopped into the leather seat in front of her own desk, which was scattered with various papers, among them the OmniGenetics ad. "Something is bugging me, but I can't put my finger on it." She picked up the ad and examined it for the hundredth time.

"Monica, how well do you know Jackie?"

"Somewhat."

"She's young. Juggling everything by herself."

"If I could just remember." She pinched the bridge of her nose and closed her eyes.

"What do you know about her?"

"Who, Jackie?" She swiveled the chair and looked at her husband.

"Hmmm."

"The mother was immature, did her own thing and left her daughter on her own a lot, didn't seem to care about her. When Jackie was young, her father did some jail time, not sure why. Jackie was fourteen when the father took off to Vegas. Then she started shoplifting, probably to get attention, and that landed her in juvenile court. A judge assigned her to the Annie Sullivan School, where Zoey was her teacher, more like a mother to her, really. No brothers and sisters."

"I hate to ask this, but could she have harmed Will?"

"I don't know, guess it's possible. I do know she worked damn hard to get her life together with all kinds of support from Zoey."

"I've sent an e-mail to all our subscribers about the abduction. Maybe someone knows something." Kurt stood up. "I'm hungry. Shall I scramble some egg whites with tomatoes and onions? Over toast?"

"Good idea. Be right out."

He headed for the kitchen; she put down the bowl of strawberries, and began to sort through the material piled in front of her. She picked up a manila envelope she didn't recognize and, when she checked the return address, felt a shock. "International Adoption Agency."

She didn't blame Kurt for mixing the envelope in with the rest of the papers, since the last time he'd tried to discuss the idea with her, she had gone ballistic. After the miscarriage, he had been spooked, afraid he would lose her if they tried again. The doctor had told them it was caused by complications from her Type 1 diabetes, terrible words. Remembering her pregnancy, a heaviness settled over her. Sure, it had been difficult, lying in bed for weeks with her blood sugar fluctuating wildly, but she yearned for their own biological child and would settle for nothing less. She yanked the top drawer open, jammed in the envelope and slammed it shut.

The smell of sautéing onions and tomatoes drifted from the kitchen, and her mouth watered, but she needed a few moments to calm herself before joining her husband.

When Monica entered the kitchen, Kurt was stirring in the egg whites. "If I had kidnapped a child," he said out loud, "where would I bring him?"

She pulled a stool out from under an island in the center of the kitchen and sat down. Then a glimmer of memory came to her. "Say, do you remember, about twenty years ago, a scandal about selling children?"

"My dear, twenty years ago, if my nose wasn't buried in a text book, I was editing the high school newspaper."

"No, really Kurt. You *must* remember." She pulled at her hair. "What was it?"

"Sorry, I don't." He placed two plates and forks on the counter. "Wouldn't it be safer to pull a car up next to a child? Force him in? Not risk going into an apartment."

"Maybe someone wanted him specifically."

"But who and why?"

She tapped her fingers on the counter. "I'm sure the police are covering that angle."

Kurt divided the eggs between the two plates. Preoccupied with their own thoughts, they ate in silence.

Suddenly, Monica jumped up and grabbed her car keys from a hook by the door. "I'll catch you at dinner," she said and dashed out the door.

CHAPTER 8

Joey LeBrun woke up thinking about Dara Lee, like he did every morning. And today she was driving him and Blake to work because his older brother's truck was at Jake's garage.

As he sat at the end of the couch which served as his bed, he began pulling on his cowboy boots with the two inch built-in lifts that brought his height to five foot four, still two inches shorter than Dara Lee. He heard the water in the bathroom shower shut off and, soon after, Blake appeared in the living room with a towel knotted around his waist, drying his hair with another.

"Fat chance I have with Dara Lee when you're hanging around looking like some damn movie star," With a final shove, Joey's foot slipped into his boot; then he stood and stamped his feet, coaxing the cuffs on his jeans to fall over his boots.

"Told you, I'm not interested."

Joey opened the closet and took out the sweater with the stripes that made his sloping shoulders appear wider. "Yeah, yeah. I get it. As long as Jackie Ravinski is alive, she'll be the steak; Dara Lee is just a side of fries."

"You know I'm a one woman guy."

"Sure don't act like it."

"Not that again. Come on, I told you I'm friendly with everyone. It's just my nature."

Joey turned toward his brother and pulled on the sweater. "You sure your relationship with Dara doesn't go past..." He indicated quotation marks with his fingers, "...friendly?" Where the hell did Blake come from anyway? Nobody else in the family looked like a goddamned Greek god.

"There's nothing between me and Dara Lee. Besides, I told you, she will flirt with anything in pants."

"You're full of shit. She likes me. I know she does."

Blake chuckled. "Well, you do wear pants."

Joey's jaw tightened, and he pressed his tongue against his teeth. "Speaking of one woman, I haven't seen Jackie around lately." He knew he was goading Blake, but he couldn't help himself. "What's with that?"

"Nothing. We're both busy. That's all."

Joey heard the pain in his brother's voice and regretted bringing it up. "Sorry." After all, when kids in the school playground had bullied him and he had run home in tears, Blake had dealt with the idiots.

But Joey wondered what had happened between Jackie and Blake. After Guy Falcone went to prison, his brother had pursued her constantly. Torn between her loyalty to Will's father and Blake's persistence, she had finally given in to his brother. They were constantly together for over three years, and Joey had never seen his brother so happy. When Blake had spent a fortune, which he didn't have, on a diamond and proposed, Jackie had backed off, asked for time to decide. They had seen less of each other. However, in the last few weeks, Jackie hadn't been around at all. Now Joey was hoping like hell that Blake wouldn't rebound with Dara Lee.

"You sure your truck'll be ready today or will Dara Lee be driving us tomorrow?" Joey examined himself in a mirror. His best sweater and it wouldn't make any difference. Not one bit. And his ears, sticking out like that. When he was wealthy he was going to have them fixed, pinned back. For the millionth time, he pressed his hands against his ears and checked himself in the mirror. If he wasn't good-looking, he'd have to make the big bucks. That would bring the women around, especially Dara Lee. He'd buy her all sorts of things: jewelry, clothes, whatever she wanted, nothing would be out of his reach.

"It's only an oil change." Blake placed his foot on a chair and began drying between his toes.

At the age of twenty-two, Joey shared this apartment with Blake, which also meant having to tolerate his father dropping in unannounced, talking about sports. Fat lot of good it did for Joey to look like his father, who preferred his older brother, anyway.

Blake snapped the wet towel at Joey. "Let me know when she's here." He disappeared into the bedroom.

Joey shut the closet door and slumped on the sofa.

He remembered a day when he was a kid in fourth grade, a week before school got out for the summer. His father had been lounging in an armchair reading a newspaper. Joey had run into the room carrying a leaflet. "Dad, my teacher said I should take this class in summer school. She said I'm really good." He held up a drawing of a pair of cardinals perched on a bird house. One affectionately touched the other with its beak.

His father had closed the newspaper, looked at his son's work, and read the notice. Frowning, he said, "Expensive."

"I can rake leaves, and in winter, I'll shovel snow. I'll pay you back."

His father had snapped open the paper and had begun to read again. "Art is for sissies. No son of mine will be an artist."

Since that day, Joey had hidden his wound and his sketch book from everyone. He longed to share it with someone, and he dreamed Dara Lee would be that person.

And Joey had plans that he kept to himself, plans that would make him rich. Someday he would show everyone that he was no loser. When a horn beeped outside, he jumped up. "She's here," he yelled in to Blake.

"Be right out."

Joey was already out the door.

When he burst from the front door, Dara Lee was lipsticking her mouth in the rearview mirror of her lime green Jetta convertible. Once, Joey had briefly wondered how she could afford such a car. The canvas top was down, and the neck of her blouse hung low, revealing lots of cleavage. Damn, she was built. Joey could not help staring. "Hey, bad boy," she said, when he slid into the passenger seat. Her hair looked bed-tousled.

She turned toward him, leaned over and fingered a black stripe on his sweater. "Ooooh... soft. Is it new, sugar?" Joey resisted the urge to kiss her; instead, he said, "Yeah, like it?"

"Hmmm, she said, fingering the material for another moment. Then she sat erect, straightened the mirror, and pulled a pack of gum from over the visor. She unwrapped a stick, folded it into her mouth, and tossed the wrapping onto the sidewalk. A door banged shut. "There he is now," she said, too enthusiastically, as far as Joey was concerned. Her cheeks were flushed.

His brother raced down the walkway, a Home Depot vest over his arm, flopping with his steps, his t-shirt pulling tight across his chest. Showing off, Joey thought, as Blake leapt into the back seat. Even from the front, Joey could smell his aftershave.

Dara Lee twisted toward Blake, laid her arm on top of her seat, and caressed the fabric with her hand. "Morning, handsome. How's the job going?"

Joey felt his eye twitch.

"Same old, same old. Staff's like children, and upper management is always bitching about something." He winked at her. "But hey, that's life in the big box world." His eyes slid toward Joey, the smile faded, and he sank back into his seat.

She turned back around, snapped her gum, and drove to the end of Allerton Street where she stopped at the intersection. Morning traffic was heavy.

"How's your job going?"

She sighed. "You know how it goes, handsome. Season's winding down. Tourists are mostly gone. Tips are in the toilet."

"Anybody'd be lucky to have you wait on them."

"Why that's so sweet, Joey, but then you're always like that, sugar pie."

"Hey, did you hear? I got a promotion."

"Promotion? More money, Joey?"

"Yep."

"Congrats." She reached over and patted his knee. He could smell the sweetness of the gum. There was a break in the traffic so she turned onto Court Street.

"His boss knows a good thing when she sees it," Blake said. "She's opening another day care center, so she needs someone reliable to run the old place. He's in charge now."

"Won't be much of a change. She's never there much. The staff pretty much runs the center."

"Don't be so modest." Dara Lee turned onto a narrow road that wound behind Cole Elementary School. Where a sign pointed to Teddy Bear Day Care, she turned into a driveway. The road continued past the Day Care and ended at a two-story brick building. "What's up there?"

"The Sunny Days," Joey said.

"Oh, so that's where the old folks live." She parked in a lot in front of a playground surrounded by a chain link fence.

Squealing, three toddlers chased each other on asphalt. Another child climbed steps to a slide, and two staff members watched the activity as they chatted. One spotted Joey and waved.

Dara Lee turned to him. "You late?"

"Nah. Some parents pay extra to drop their kids off early."

At the end of the parking lot, a woman emerged from a Victorian house. As soon as the two young staffers spotted her, they separated; one moved closer to the boy on the slide, the other nearer to the toddlers. The woman strode to the car. "Good morning," she said to no one in particular. Her cheek bones and cinnamon eyes were striking, but there was a coldness about her.

"My boss, Gwendolyn Grey," said Joey. She nodded absently at Dara Lee, but her eyes brightened when she noticed Blake in the back seat. "Good to see you again." Mechanically, she turned to Joey. "There's a problem and we need to talk." Without waiting for him to reply, she started back to the house. Her hair, dark and braided, was tied at the bottom with a crimson ribbon, and it swayed as she glided across the lawn. Joey scrambled from the car and hurried after her.

"Hey, I'm no chauffeur. Up here, handsome. "Dara Lee patted the passenger seat, so Blake moved into the front. "What time is work?"

"Not until one o'clock."

"What!? It's 7:30 in the morning."

"So? I was planning on hanging out in the garage with Jake, then heading over to work early."

"Impress the boss, huh?" She snapped her gum. "I've got a better idea. Hang out with me instead. Grab coffee at Starbucks. Maybe later, lunch at the Union Fish Restaurant. Get your truck after that." She flipped her hair. "I'm a lot prettier than Jake, and lots more fun." At first he thought of how Joey would feel, but then, what he didn't know couldn't hurt him. He laughed and agreed.

CHAPTER 9

Joey hustled after his boss with a mixture of feelings: a twinge of regret at having to leave Dara Lee, especially with his brother as a passenger, and anxiety about the problem his boss had mentioned. Had he screwed up in some way? It was hard to read Gwendolyn—or "Miss Grey" as she expected to be called. He followed behind on the path that led to the Victorian house, but she was tall and her stride was long and quick, so he lagged behind. He watched her braid and the crimson ribbon sway with her steps. Her hair hung far below her waist.

After entering her office, Joey chose a seat as far away from her as possible and crossed his arms. Sitting ramrod straight, she tapped a pencil on her desk, where everything was arranged as if aligned by an invisible grid: the letter tray was parallel to the edge of the desk, as was her laptop. A stack of Post-it notes was equidistant between the phone and pen holder. When he was settled, she put down the pencil and folded her hands.

She inclined her head slightly to the left as she spoke. Joey supposed that move was intended to make her look softer, more friendly. To him, it appeared contrived and mechanical. "I understand the children are interacting with the residents at the nursing home."

Joey unfolded his arms and relaxed. Whew! He hadn't screwed up. "The old folks get a kick out of them. At the end of the day, when it's nice enough, they sit outside. Most watch the kids play. A few talk to them."

"It has to stop."

He blinked several times, then frowned. "I don't understand. The kids don't bother them. And staff members are always with them."

She waved her hand in dismissal.

"The owner didn't complain, did he? He's out there occasionally. Seems like a nice fellow."

She cleared her throat. "This is not about the owner, either."

"Are you concerned about safety? Those patients are really elderly. They can't possibly harm anyone, if that's what you're thinking."

She snickered, then caught herself. "Hardly."

"Can I ask why? You know, so I can explain it to the staff."

She picked up the pencil and began tapping it again. Joey noticed a vein pulsing in her neck as she cleared her throat. "If you must know, it's a liability issue. Accidents do happen. I could be sued. I don't want the children near the patients." Standing, she smoothed the front of her slacks. "If necessary, keep the children inside when the residents are on the lawn." She stepped from behind her desk and Joey scrambled up. When she opened the door, she sniffed. "Do you understand?"

"Don't you worry one little bit, Miss Grey. It's already taken care of."

After the meeting, Joey was puzzled and didn't understand the big deal about the kids being around the geezers at Sunny Days. Sure, accidents happen, but the kids were supervised by staff. Besides, their antics were entertainment for the old folks, and the kids liked the attention.

His boss was an odd sort. While pulling supplies from cupboards for the day's activities—construction paper, crayons, washable paint and glue—he noticed her leaving the building rather hurriedly. Soon afterward, her BMW roared out of the parking lot. He slammed the cupboard door. "Doesn't deserve her success," he mumbled out loud. Every day, she was either shut up in her office with the door closed or nowhere to be found; certainly no way to run things. But he was glad whenever she left; without her around, everyone was at ease and the place ran smoothly. It made his job simpler.

He guessed she was busy setting up her branch center. Would she name it Teddy Bear Two? Had a ring to it. He wondered what he would he name his. When he opened his own day care center, not just one or two, but a whole string of them. He'd franchise them out. Get rich that way.

But he was frustrated, uncertain how to begin: choosing a location, obtaining permits, whatever it took. Not wanting to her pick her brain, which would make her suspicious, he had tried the next best thing, picking the lock to her office. But that had failed. However, that morning, when he passed her office carrying the plastic bin with materials for classrooms, he noticed her door was slightly ajar, which was unusual. Must have been in a real hurry this morning. Without hesitation, he placed the bin on the floor and pushed open the door. This was his chance to rummage through her stuff, steal her ideas.

At first, he stood in the room and looked around. There was nothing to soften the stark utility. No plants or photos, no paintings on the walls to add warmth. Noticing an ordinary, gray filing cabinet in a corner, he hurried over and tugged on the drawers, but they didn't budge. Perhaps she left the key in the top drawer of the desk, he thought. But, after poking through it, he found nothing but pens, paperclips, index cards and more Post-it notes. Next, he checked the papers in the letter tray, but discovered only bills for electricity, heat and other operating expenses. When he put them back, he made sure he stacked them as perfectly as she had done. Adjacent to the tray was a plain, sealed envelope, waiting for a stamp. It was addressed to Home & Hearth Inn, a sleazy motel located near the old cordage factory, the part that had not been renovated. He thought it strange that a classy woman like her would have anything to do with that place.

He heard a door slam shut and then footsteps in the corridor. He rushed out of the office, shutting the door behind him and picked up the bin. A staff member with a pony tail, wearing sweat pants and blouse with an animal print, appeared from around a corner.

"Oh, hi, Joey." She checked her watch and pointed at the bin. "Parents will be coming soon. Need some help with that?"

"Thanks, Patricia. I'd appreciate it."

Together, they entered the first classroom. Patricia scooped boxes of crayons and blunt pointed scissors from the bin. When she stepped away, Joey picked up small tubs of Play Doh.

"You know, this staff is incredible," she said, placing the materials on a table. "Everyone pulls together. Real team players. And everyone is great with the kids."

"One thing Miss Grey does well; she knows how to hire great people."

"Oh, Joey, no one likes her. If you weren't here, everyone would have quit long ago."

"I try to be fair."

"And you treat people with respect, not like that condescending bitch."

For a long time, Joey had suspected Gwendolyn's success was due to staff. If he had his own business, he was sure they would go with him. However, he was conflicted. At times he felt guilty. Even though she was odd and a cold fish, she had been good to him. The staff sure was dynamite. That is, everyone except that idiot with the flaming red hair, Todd O'Malley—lazy and late all the time, which drove Joey crazy. Possessing a quick smile, and a sense of humor, Todd got by on his charm. "I wonder why Miss Burke keeps Todd around." Joey said.

"He's not the best worker, but he makes me laugh. I like him."

When he and Patricia had finished placing supplies in each of the classrooms, he felt satisfied. He enjoyed the kids, and it was good being in charge. Since it was time for the mothers to drop off their children, they both stepped outside.

Everyone was accounted for, except, of course, Todd. One staff member was playing with the toddlers who had arrived early; the other employees stood in the drop-off zone. Joey sure could use Todd during this busy time. A Ford Galaxy pulled up, crunching gravel in the horseshoe driveway, and a woman hopped out and released a two-year-old from the car seat. The Ford left and a Lexus pulled in, followed by a Fiat.

A movement caught Joey's attention. Someone sprinted across the lawn and disappeared behind the nursing home. Joey recognized the red hair. What the hell was Todd up to now?

CHAPTER 10

Zoey was surprised to see her sister rush into the police station. Monica hesitated and her eyes widened before she approached Zoey and David. "Well, hello there," she said to him, as her gaze shifted to his hand resting on Zoey's knee. "Certainly didn't expect to see you two together."

"Good to see you again, Monica." He said.

"Likewise." She turned to her sister. "I wanted to ask you something."

David stood and rubbed the back of his head. "Well, I haven't had breakfast yet."

Monica placed her hand on her chest. "Don't leave on my account."

He smiled at Zoey. "Be back in a bit." He nodded his head once at Monica and walked out of the building.

"What's up with that?" Monica waved her hand in the direction of David's retreat.

"Nothing."

"Doesn't look like nothing." Monica's tone was mocking, and Zoey could see the beginning of a smirk.

Zoey crossed her arms. "You wanted to ask me something?"

Monica settled into in the chair David had left and stretched out her legs. "Do you remember a story about someone selling children? About twenty years ago? You were around twelve. I had just graduated from high school."

Zoey frowned, trying to remember, then shook her head. "Sorry, I don't. Weren't you taking a course in journalism that summer?"

"I was."

"Are you thinking someone took Will to sell him?"

"Don't know. It's worth a shot." Monica rubbed her chin. "Police are doing everything else possible. Can't just sit and do nothing."

"You know, last night, I woke up with a bad feeling. A dread, really. I knew something was happening."

"One of your intuitions."

"Yeah." Zoey unfolded her arms, leaned forward and stared down at the floor. "Twenty years ago. That was the summer Dad left, wasn't it?"

"That was the summer, all right."

"You were working two jobs, saving money for college. And taking that journalism course. It was damn hot and humid that year. I remember that."

"Miserable. In more ways than one." Monica sighed.

"I came home that afternoon and wondered why Dad's car wasn't in the driveway."

"Oh, that's right. I'd forgotten. He was working the night shift then. Should have been home sleeping."

Zoey sighed. "I opened the front door and the smell of beer was so strong. It made gag. And those bottles all over the living room floor. Mom sprawled on the couch."

"I got home just before you. I tried so hard to get her up. Have her drink coffee. Walk it off. Anything. But she wouldn't budge."

Zoey felt sadness creep up from some dark place. "I'll never forget her words." She looked at her sister.

"You asked her where Daddy was."

"Yup. She said, 'He's gone and won't be back. Never. Ever.'" Zoey felt a shadow of the shame and disgust that she had felt back then. "She started flinging her arms around like she was swatting at flies."

"In a way, I wish he'd never gotten sober."

"Why would you want that?"

"Then he wouldn't have left us."

"That's crazy, Monica. I understand he couldn't live with mom's drinking anymore. But did he have to desert us too? We didn't do anything wrong."

"It was the only way he could handle it."

Zoey scowled and turned in her chair to face her sister. "Stop defending him. You always do that. We needed him. He was a grown man with kids."

She realized her voice was loud and was glad there was no one else in the lobby with them.

Monica glared at her. Her mouth opened and closed, but nothing came out. She bolted out of her seat, took a few steps with her back to her sister, hesitated and then whirled around. "You just don't get it, but you never did." With a huff, she barged out of the police station.

Zoey took a deep breath. Confrontations with Monica always felt abrasive as sandpaper. She realized, at times, her own impulsive reactions brought them on, but that knowledge didn't make her feel any better. Often, she wondered if these blowups somehow protected both of them. After all, if they never became close again, they would never talk about their baby brother. Never have to face his death or their guilt.

That summer night, so long ago, with the temperature close to one hundred, Zoey remembered she had been sweating, unable to sleep. The bedroom window was wide open, but the curtains hung limply because there was no breeze. Her sheets were drenched with sweat, as was her long t-shirt.

From the bedroom across the hall, her baby brother began crying for his midnight feeding. "Monica, wake up." It was her sister's turn to care for him. But when Zoey had rolled over, she'd seen that Monica's bed was empty. She had gone out with friends and wasn't back yet.

So Zoey had hauled herself from bed and stumbled down the stairs. Grateful that a bottle of formula was left in the refrigerator, she made a mental note to buy more Similac in the morning. After heating up his bottle and testing it on her wrist, she entered his bedroom where her mother was snoring. The alcohol stench was worse because of the heat.

He was only wearing a diaper. When Zoey had lifted her brother from his crib, he was sweating. She checked his diaper; he was okay. While cradling him in one arm and feeding him his bottle with the other, she hummed softly as she listened to the sucking noises he made. She loved the way he fixated on her face, the way he wrapped his whole hand around her pinky finger and, of course, that new baby smell. Glad that Monica was consumed with her own life, Zoey looked after her brother. That was the happiest she had ever been. Zoey, at the age of twelve, had become his caregiver.

After placing him back in the crib and winding up the mobile attached to the side railing, she'd been overcome by a feeling of dread; she knew something awful was about to happen. That night she'd stayed in the chair next to the crib and had fallen asleep listening to *Twinkle, Twinkle, Little Star.*

The doctors had called it Sudden Infant Death Syndrome, or SIDS, and said no one was to blame, but Zoey blamed herself. After all, she was the one who was looking after him. Surely, she must have done something wrong to cause the death of her little brother. As she had grown older, she came to a more realistic understanding, but the pain of that loss had never fully healed. Although Monica never admitted anything, Zoey knew her sister blamed herself. After all, she was the older sister and it had been her turn to care for him.

Closing her eyes, Zoey leaned her head against the wall. She felt like an island swamped by a hurricane, just as she had twenty years ago.

CHAPTER 11

Stuck in a line of traffic behind an accident on Route 3, Todd O'Malley laughed hysterically at the flurry of activity. A Patriots cap partially covered his brilliant red hair. His jeans, ripped at the knee, needed a good washing and so did his shirt. He liked wearing grunge clothing and shopped at the local Salvation Army.

A few cars in front of him, a horse trailer transporting a herd of goats had struck a flatbed truck. Several crates of live chickens had fallen off the flatbed and broken open. Also, the door of the horse trailer had flown open releasing the goats. Neither the animals nor the drivers were injured, not that Todd would have cared, but goats were bleating and jumping, and chickens were squawking and flapping. A cloud of feathers grew larger with each moment. The road was completely blocked by the trailer and truck. Traffic was rapidly backing up.

Occupants of a few of the cars were scrambling to help catch the animals. One woman in a wool shawl and slacks had bent over to grab a chicken, when one of the goats butted her in the behind and sent her sprawling. Good thing none of those goats had horns, Todd thought, or if they had, perhaps it would have been more fun to watch.

Scrambling to catch their animals, both truck drivers were cursing. One was holding a chicken upside down by its legs, as the bird attempted to peck him. The other man held a screaming goat under each arm as he marched back to the trailer.

A limousine with a flat tire had pulled over and a bridal party was outside. Two bridesmaids in chartreuse, strapless gowns were doubled over with laughter, a third was shooing a chicken away from her hem, and the bride stood in her lace gown with one hand over her mouth. Her other hand held her bouquet straight down at her side. She was unaware of the goat standing beside and slightly behind her, nibbling her flowers.

Eventually, the police arrived, sirens blaring and lights whirling; some cops helped to round up the escapees, although many had disappeared. Other officers directed traffic around the mess, and Todd managed to arrive late to work at the Teddy Bear Day Care. But, first, he had some business of his own to conduct. He parked one street away and snuck to the side of the building where he was able to check on his boss, Joey LeBrun. When Todd saw that Joey had his back to him, he raced across the lawn and hid behind the Sunny Days nursing home.

As he stood between two windows at the rear of the home, Todd O'Malley figured Joey had not spotted him. The morning was chilly with a slight breeze. Vigorously rubbing his arms, he regretted not having worn his jacket. Then he chuckled, remembering the slogan on the back of the t-shirt he was wearing: "Chill Out."

None of the residents would be in the dining room yet. One of the two cooks would be getting breakfast ready. He hoped to hell it wouldn't be Guy's mother. If he ran the place, workers would have the same predictable schedule every week, so they could plan their free time better. He never understood why the owner switched the days and hours around so much.

The nurse on duty, along with the assistants, would be passing out medications and helping patients to the bathroom. He wondered if Becky and Jackie were working. Usually, they had the same shift. Both were always pleasant when he brought the children up on the back lawn to play. With those two women, he always turned on the charm. He could do that when he wanted, like flipping on a light switch. Todd didn't bother with Gwendolyn because she needed him and he knew it.

He sidled over to the kitchen window where he could see the cook. Luck was with him: it wasn't Guy's mother. Laura was young and she could be pretty, but she didn't take care of herself. If her nail polish wasn't chipped, then her eye makeup was smudged. And her breath smelled like last week's dinner.

Todd tapped on the pane and her head snapped toward the sound. When she saw him, he grinned and waved. She placed a spatula on a counter, turned off the heat under a frying pan filled with sliced potatoes, and hurried to open the window. Since he had not eaten, the smell of hash browns cooking made his stomach grumble.

She wiped her nose with her finger. "Got two?"

He pulled two glassine packets from his pocket and she retrieved a twenty dollar bill from her apron.

"Missus Falcone told me to give you a message." He cocked his head to the side. "She don't want you coming 'round here no more." He squeezed his eyebrows together, looking puzzled, as if this were the first time he'd heard this message.

Guy's mother was beginning to be a nuisance. And now she was telling other people. "What's the problem?" he asked, as if anxious to know.

"She don't care what you did before this. But her son Guy is outta prison now."

"So?"

"She don't want the cops to connect you with the place she works. That might cause more trouble for her son than he already has. That's the message."

Todd felt a tightening in his chest, and a sour feeling in his stomach. Damn! His Tums were back in his glove compartment. Guy's mother probably figured that he owed them because Guy hadn't testified against him when he got caught dealing. But the mother could cause trouble for him. Real trouble—if she told the owner of the nursing home about him selling drugs on his property, or worse, if she told the cops.

She sniffed. "So how about me? If you don't come 'round no more, where am I gonna find you?"

He'd have to figure something out. He flashed a smile. "Not to worry. I wouldn't want to lose a good customer like you."

From a hallway, he heard footsteps heading for the kitchen. She slammed the window shut, and he moved away to the end of the building. Chatter and laughter drifted from the day care. When he peered around the corner, a procession of automobiles was dropping off children. He spotted Joey talking with a parent.

Shit! Gwendolyn's car was not there. He ducked his head back behind the building. Risky to carry her packets around until she decided to show up. Who knew when the bitch would be back? But then, he was later than he'd intended to be because of the accident, so what could he expect?

He stuck his head out again. Joey was looking around, so he ducked back. Even though Joey was easygoing with the staff, Todd knew Joey did not like him; he bristled when Todd was late or didn't do his share of the work. Although he didn't care what Joey thought of him, Todd hated confrontation, and Joey had spoken to him once already. Not that Gwendolyn would ever fire him. Fat chance! Where else would she get her drugs, and his discretion? Again, Todd peeked around the corner. This time, Joey's back was turned, so he rushed across the lawn and joined the other staff members who were greeting clients. An Audi drove in and he put on his best smile.

CHAPTER 12

Part of the Union Fish Raw Bar and Restaurant was a deck where lunch could be enjoyed with a view of the Plymouth Yacht Club. A plastic roof supported by poles permitted customers to sit outside, even on rainy days.

Blake sat and fidgeted, uncomfortable with his back to the room, but it had been the last available table and Dara Lee wouldn't wait for another one. He cricked his neck right, then left, and checked his watch. Noon, still plenty of time to get his truck from the garage and punch in at Home Depot.

Jackie must be working. He imagined her dressed in scrubs, helping some elderly woman at the nursing home. How he ached for her. That bitch, Zoey Stone, had pushed her to train as a Certified Nurse's Aide, but Jackie didn't need to work at all because he would take care of her. He was sure that Stone was behind Jackie's cooling off toward him; he was determined to show her and everyone else that Jackie belonged to him. The sooner people realized that, the better off everyone would be.

The bill had been paid; the table was cleared. Where the hell was Dara Lee? Still in the bathroom? He turned in his chair, looked around and spotted her leaning against the bar, talking to a man in a leather jacket. Blake squinted and blinked. What the hell? It couldn't be!

He was on his feet, fists clenched, before he was even aware of getting up. Guy Falcone was drinking a Budweiser and listening to Dara Lee. As Blake stormed toward them, Falcone caught sight of him and tightened his grip on the bottle. Simultaneously, Dara Lee spotted Blake. Her smile dissolved into a scowl, and she thrust her arms out to stop him. "Hey, what're you doing?"

He pushed her arms away and stepped past her. Halting within a foot of Falcone, he snarled, "You bastard! What the fuck you doing here? Thought you had more time."

Guy drained the last of his beer, his eyes hard on Blake. "Time? Got plenty of that."

"How'd you get out?"

"Turned the knob and pushed."

"Don't be a fucking wise ass." His muscles were taut. "Stay away from Jackie."

"You low-life shit. I heard about you and Jackie." Guy inched toward him, so close that Blake smelled the beer on his breath. The bartender stopped wiping a glass, and customers began to notice. "Will's my son," said Guy in a loud voice, poking his finger in Blake's chest. "My ma and me—we got rights."

Dara Lee moved toward the exit. "C'mon Blake. Time for work," she urged, but he didn't budge. "Your ride is leaving."

He heard her voice quiver. Blake smirked and lied, "Jackie and I are getting married."

Guy exploded from his seat. He grabbed Blake's shirt and slammed him against the bar. "Mother-fucker!" Pain shot up Blake's back. Customers scrambled away, knocking over chairs. The bartender frantically jabbed numbers into a phone. At the same time, Dara Lee yelled, "Oh, God, no! Guy, don't."

Shaking uncontrollably, Blake held up his hands in surrender. But Guy didn't let go until Blake heard Dara Lee, "I beg you! Stop! Puhleez!" He could tell she was crying. Guy must have known too, because he let go.

In the parking lot, Dara Lee gulped in air and leaned against her car. Blake was bent over with his hands on his knees, breathing hard. Finally, she climbed in and started the car. A few moments later he scrambled into the passenger seat and tried joking, "Leaving without me?"

"Hadn't decided." She pulled away from the restaurant.

When she stopped for a light, she reached above the visor, pulled out a pack of gum, and unwrapped two sticks. Blake noticed her hands were shaking.

"I've never seen you like that." She stuffed gum into her mouth and tossed the wrappers onto the street.

"He's the reason that Jackie's been putting me off."

"Hon, Jackie didn't know he'd been released."

"You don't know that." His voice was low.

"I'm her best friend. Remember? And *I* sure as hell didn't know he was out." The light turned green, so she pressed down on the gas pedal and accelerated fast.

Blake braced himself against on the dashboard. "God damn it. Will's his *son.* That means he'll *have* to see Jackie." He felt bile rise from his stomach, burning on the way up.

"You knew Will was his son when you started dating her."

"Yah, but he was locked up then."

"It isn't about him, anyway. Sweetie, she told you why she's backing off."

He slammed his fist into the dashboard. "What's wrong with wanting to marry her?"

"Calm down, will you?" She slowed as she passed the front of Jake's garage and turned into the driveway, churning dust into the air. She pulled into the lot and parked. Blake's truck was out back already. The garage had two bays; one was rolled open.

"It wasn't about marriage. She felt you were too controlling and she told you that. She needs time, so give her some space."

He didn't know how to do that. Feeling helpless and panicked, and unable to tolerate such feelings, he bolted from her Jetta and hurried toward the garage as if he could outrun his demons.

Inside the garage, he smelled gasoline and oil and heard clanking from under an antique Ford Thunderbird. He bent down. "Jake, you under there?"

The noise stopped. "Just a sec." Clinking continued for another minute, and then Jake rolled out on a creeper, stood and pulled a rag from the back pocket of his overalls. Straps attached to the back stretched over his shoulders and hooked over large buttons on a bib in front. Should cut that hair, Blake thought, looking at the long gray strands that were pulled back and secured with a rubber band at the nape of his neck.

"Truck's ready," he said, wiping his hands as he walked to a table shoved against a wall.

He followed. Jake shuffled through papers, found the one he wanted, and handed Blake a bill. Dara Lee caught up to them. After sticking a toothpick in his mouth, Jake leaned against the table and looked her over. "Honey, you're due for a checkup."

"And you know you'll get it." She managed a grin and leaned toward him. "The Jetta, that is."

A tabby cat darted into the garage, jumped on the trunk of the Thunderbird, flicked its tail and kneaded its claws on the finish. "Damn cat." Jake grabbed for it, but it dodged him and scampered under the Ford. Dara Lee laughed. Already Jake was on the floor peering under the car. "C'mon Peaches." He tapped the floor repeatedly with his fingers, encouraging the cat to come out, but it stubbornly remained where it was.

Dara Lee went to the opposite side of the Ford. "Help us, Blake." He shrugged his shoulders and held his palms up toward the ceiling. "How?" She pointed to the front of the car. "Try standing there. Peaches might scoot out that way." Dara Lee disappeared from his sight when she crouched down on her hands and knees. So Blake walked to the front, knelt down and looked under. When he saw Jake with his arm extended underneath the chaise, snapping his fingers to attract Peaches' attention, and Dara Lee cooing to the cat, he laughed out loud. Peaches was hunkered down, ignoring both, happily licking her paw. Just after Blake straightened up and wiped off his knees, the cat darted by him and stood in the open bay. Another cat appeared next to Peaches, all black except for a white tip on its tail. That cat stretched out its legs as it pushed its butt in the air. Then it sat next to Peaches and began to lick her ear.

By then, Jake and Dara Lee were back on their feet. Jake said, "Bad cat," but Blake heard the affection in his voice. In response, Peaches meowed at Jake as if letting him know who was in charge. Then, followed by the other cat, Peaches marched from the garage with her tail held high.

CHAPTER 13

After Monica left the police station in a huff, Zoey remained seated alone in the lobby. She picked at her fingernails as she waited. Jackie's interview was taking too long. Down the corridor she heard raised voices, and somewhere a door slammed. Before long, Tom Madsen appeared from a corridor at the rear of the lobby with his mouth tightened into a thin line. When he noticed her, he raised his eyebrows, and approached. "Oh, you're still here."

"What's going on? Is Jackie all right?"

"She's okay, I was just with her and Dalbeck. Still being interviewed.

"What? Still! What the hell's going on?"

"Sure you want to wait?"

She nodded.

"She'll be here for a stretch." He checked his watch. "Just after ten. You definitely have plenty of time to grab a coffee or something to eat."

"I'll wait." Zoey crossed her arms. "Any news on Will?"

Madsen shook his head.

She took a deep breath. "I am hungry. Haven't eaten anything today."

"I have to get back."

"Say Tom, Jackie leaves a spare key in her flower pot. Such an obvious place. Anybody wanting to break in would look there. Might as well put the damn key smack in the door lock. But my point is, did the police find that key, or is it still in the pot?"

"I'll check to see what was found."

"If it's still in the pot, it might implicate Jackie. But if it's missing, doesn't that point to someone breaking in?"

"I'll look into it."

Two officers appeared from the corridor and entered the lobby. One was tall with narrow eyes. The other was Asian and addressed Madsen, "Ready?"

"Gotta go," Lightly, Madsen squeezed her arm. "I miss seeing you with David." He grimaced, turned and walked into the street with the two men.

Because Friendly's was a two-minute walk from the police station, Zoey decided to head over there.

CHAPTER 14

The unexpected thunderstorm had moved out to sea, but the sky remained overcast, so the convertible top on Becky Carlin's VW Beetle was up. But the weather didn't dampen her mood as she drove up Route 3 from Quincy.

Such fun these past few days, she thought. Maggie was a hoot. At eighty years young, her grandmother's only concession to age was a cane. Both women were tall and thin, but unlike her, Becky had never outgrown her gawkiness. At the age of thirty-two, she figured she never would.

She remembered sitting side by side playing slots at Foxwoods. Maggie with her lucky Red Sox cap, banging her cane on the floor every time the machine set off a winning bing-bing-bing. And last night, staying overnight in Quincy, Becky had listened to her fortune as Maggie flipped over the Tarot cards. Of course, Becky would become famous and wealthy, marry a prince and travel everywhere.

Smiling, she turned off Exit 5 and sighed. One more day off, then it's back to nursing at Sunny Days. The familiar loneliness settled in. She decided to soothe that feeling with comfort food—ice cream and a cheeseburger at Friendly's. It was too late to be called breakfast, too early to be lunch, but what did that matter? Comfort food was for anytime.

Ten minutes later, when she pulled into the parking lot, she saw Zoey opening the front door. By the time she'd parked and entered the building, her friend was seated in a booth examining a menu. She hurried over, Zoey spotted her, and they hugged. After they ordered cheeseburgers and Cokes, Zoey filled her in about Will, the search for him, Jackie's interrogation, and Guy Falcone's release. Becky was devastated.

"I can't believe this. He's such a little guy. Poor Jackie." Becky shook her head. "You know, I've gotten to know her pretty well since we've worked together. She's terrific. Best nurse's aide I've ever worked with. The old folks love her. She's certainly had more than her share to deal with. I admire how she's handled it."

"She is special, even if she doesn't always see it."

The waitress delivered their burgers and Cokes. Zoey stirred her drink with the straw, clinking ice against the glass. "Say, Monica was asking me about a story from twenty years ago. Something about children being sold. Do you remember anything about that?"

Becky pursed her lips for a moment. "Can't think of anything. Is it important?

Zoey shrugged. "Don't know."

"That's the summer the two of you spent with me. Remember? At my grandmother's house?" Becky bit into her cheeseburger.

"Every weekend. That was so much fun. Swimming at Wollaston Beach, playing cards." Zoey laughed. "Especially eating all that ice cream." She sipped her drink. "You know, the best part was, I could forget about the problems at home, if only for a little while. I was so young back then. At the time I was too young to realize that Maggie was helping us get through that awful summer. I can never thank your grandmother enough."

"Me either. You became my best friend that summer."

"Same for me." Zoey smiled at her. "Remember that horseshoe crab we found on the beach?"

"The one with the broken tail?"

"Yeah. Monica was so repulsed by it."

"I don't remember that."

"You know, she became kinda like that crab."

"How so?"

"Hard on the outside. She can't expose her soft underbelly. It's not safe."

"My grandmother once said that Monica became flamboyant to attract the attention she needed."

"Yet she pretends she doesn't even want it."

They finished the burgers and Zoey checked her watch. She decided she had time to order ice cream with her friend. "Say, Can you do me a favor?"

"Anything," Becky said.

"Could you go to Jackie's apartment and see if the spare key is in her flower pot at the bottom of her steps?"

CHAPTER 15

Dara Lee dropped Blake off at Home Depot. As he walked toward the store, she ogled him while imagining them in an embrace. And, eager to keep her chances with him alive, she returned to the Union Fish Raw Bar and Restaurant. However, Guy Falcone was no longer there, which made sense. He had caused a scene there. Driving around Plymouth, she checked the parking lots of bars until she found his motorcycle in front of the Ninety-Nine Restaurant.

Inside, he was watching sports on TV. While he drank his beer, she slid onto a stool next to him. "Hey, bad boy."

He grinned. "Haven't changed much, have you?"

"What? And wreck a good thing?" Dara Lee recognized the bartender and waved to him.

"Bloody Mary?"

"Why yes," she said, pleased that he remembered her drink, but why wouldn't he? She was sure he was attracted to her, like all men. She rewarded him by giving him her best smile and stretched for a dish of pretzels, displaying her cleavage in the process. Assured he'd gotten an eyeful, she turned to Guy. "Prison hasn't changed you. Still have that manly appeal."

Guy shook his head. "Don't ever want to spend any fucking time there again."

"Jackie missed you something awful."

"That so?"

"Of course. You two had a good thing." The bartender placed her drink on a napkin.

"A good thing, huh?" He focused on her with narrowed eyes. "So why'd she stop visiting me?"

Dara Lee knew exactly why. Blake had come on strong, and Jackie was conflicted. She was falling for Blake. And why not? Drop dead gorgeous, charming, good job. "It was too painful for her to see you in prison. You know how sensitive she is. And she had Will to take care of, so she had to put him first. She loved you, still does."

"Wouldn't be putting me on, would you?"

"Now what possible reason would I have for doing that? I happen to believe families belong together."

Guy was silent for a long time and stared at his beer. "She's getting married, isn't she?"

She snorted. "Nope, but Blake would like you to believe that."

"You're telling me there's no other guy?"

"None." It wasn't really a lie, Dara Lee thought. Jackie was taking a break from Blake, sorting things out. "What I think you should do is—"

Guy interrupted her. "Hey bartender, turn that up." Annoyance shot up Dara Lee's spine. What the hell was screwing up her strategy? She looked up. The television was displaying a photo of Will in a corner of the screen while a female reporter with brilliant white teeth was speaking. "The mother of this six-year-old boy is a suspect in his abduction." Dara Lee set down her drink as a chill swept through her.

The scene shifted location to a field behind the old cordage factory. A male reporter, gray hair blowing in the wind, began talking. "Will has been missing from his home since last night."

Good God, this can't be real.

"In spite of a massive effort," he continued, "there are no clues as to the child's whereabouts. Searches have been conducted in vacant lots throughout the area. A new search is about to get underway near Ropewalk Court." A helicopter was heard overhead. The camera panned past people milling around, then swept across a field that was thick with bushes, grasses and trees choked with vines. "It doesn't appear likely that a child would be in this tangle," the reporter said, "however, every effort is being made to find him."

Guy's bar stool scraped back. His face was white; his expression grim. Was he afraid? Angry? She couldn't read him. Before she could wrap her head around any of it, he'd bolted from the bar.

CHAPTER 16

As Becky steered her VW into Jackie's driveway, she was jolted by the sight of yellow tape flapping outside the building. The reality hit her hard. Will was missing. She imagined him dancing down the steps. As she parked she noticed golden mums swaying in a flower pot at the bottom of the steps. She stepped from her car and looked more closely at the pot of flowers. The soil was disturbed, and clumps of dirt dotted the asphalt. A circular smudge appeared under the pot, indicating that it had been moved. She stuck her fingers into the dirt and felt around the edge of the pot. Nothing. After loosening the roots of the plant with her fingers, she lifted it up, placed it on the ground, and dumped out the rest of the soil. Again, nothing.

Upstairs, a window creaked open and she heard, "Who's down there?" Her stomach wrenched when she recognized the voice, but she steeled herself, stepped back down and looked up, promising herself she would remain civil. After all, the priority was finding Will.

Butch Crow, the upstairs tenant, had stuck his head out of the window. His mop of salt and pepper hair was unkempt and he needed a shave. When he saw her, he stopped scratching his neck. "Oh, it's you. Have they found her son yet?"

She shook her head.

"Whatcha doing down there?"

"The spare key. It's gone."

"So maybe she didn't put it back." He smoothed back his hair, but it still looked scruffy. "Do you wanna come up for a drink?"

"Too early for that."

"Coffee then. I'll make us coffee."

"Thought I'd join the search party."

"Search party?"

"Over by the old rope factory."

"I'll join you. Just give me a sec." His head disappeared and he slammed the window shut.

She plopped down on a step to wait and cupped her hands under her chin. Feeling hollow, she wished she were better at saying no to people. Oh well, another body looking for Will couldn't hurt. The thought comforted her a bit, but she knew it was a mistake giving him a ride. Speaking of mistakes, what a whopper she had made last year on the Fourth of July, getting drunk, which she'd never done before, just the occasional glass of wine. But that Fourth of July morning… she closed her eyes and remembered.

The smell of bacon and eggs sizzling in the pan had greeted Ken that morning as he walked into her kitchen wearing the robe he kept in her bedroom closet. "Hmmm, smells good," he had said, kissing the back of her neck as she turned over the eggs, easy, just as he liked them.

After she set his breakfast on the table, she said, "You know, we've been together just over three years."

"That long? It goes by fast when you're having fun." He had grinned at her.

"You know, my biological clock is ticking. Don't you think it's time we got married?"

He had stopped chewing and remained quiet as he finished his breakfast; she thought he was weighing his options.

Later, dressed in sweats, he fidgeted with the draw strings on his hood as he stood in the open door of her apartment.

"What's wrong?" she had asked.

She knew before he told her. Her body felt numb as if he had dumped her into a frigid pond and held her head under.

"I can't marry you." And then he had disappeared before she could respond.

Later, she discovered he had been married for the entire three years, one month and twelve days of their relationship. She considered herself to be a sensible person and felt like a fool, having missed the warning signs. Hell, looking back, the red flags had practically bashed her over the head. What lovers never see each other on weekends? Taking care of his sick mother, he had told her. Becky had swallowed it, hook, line and sinker, but his mother had been dead and buried for over a decade. It had been so easy to ignore what she did not want to see. But she had yearned for a child, a husband and a home. The rotten part was that he knew what she desired, and he had taken advantage.

So, on the night of that July Fourth, she had drained a bottle of pinot grigio in record time, while she slumped on a bench watching rippled reflections of fireworks in Plymouth Harbor. Loneliness and depression seeped in to replace her anger. It was then that she noticed a man several feet away entertaining kids by blowing up balloons that squeaked as he twisted them together, magically transforming them into animals. Some children squirmed in their parents' arms, others hopped in place, or stared wide-eyed as the man tied long ribbons onto his creations. Parents dropped dollar bills into a pail labeled TIPS FOR THE BALLOON MAN.

Through her drunken haze, Becky realized she had met that person before. Was it at a barbeque in Jackie's backyard? She thought so. He was a custodian at a mall, or some local elementary school. When he approached her with balloons shaped into a cat, she smiled up at him and he secured a ribbon around her wrist. When he kissed her cheek, her depression lifted, if only a bit. After the fireworks finished and the crowd thinned, she had invited him home and into her bed, something which she had also never done before. Sex had been perfunctory. Afterward, she'd felt lonelier than before and regretted her foolishness.

Butch Crow was taking his time. While wondering if there was some way she could back out of giving him a ride, she heard a door shut behind her.

She turned. Butch was standing on the porch with his hair slicked down. He was wearing jeans and a shirt covered with brightly colored balloons.

CHAPTER 17

After Guy roared away from the house on his motorcycle, his mother decided it was time to buy flowers for her husband's grave. He had always loved geraniums so, after running a few errands, she drove toward Walmart in her SUV. A sensitive woman, she felt hurt that Guy had criticized her purchases for Will, so she turned on the radio to try and distract herself.

Desperately, she wanted to believe that a court would grant her son custody over Jackie. Another chance with a son and, the second time around, she would raise him right. Her need was so great and her fantasy so powerful that her sense of reality had become distorted. She believed she would be raising Will.

On the radio, a meteorologist finished the weather report. Music led into local news. When she heard about her grandson, Will, being kidnapped, her hands began to shake so violently that she had to pull over to the curb to avoid an accident. Her grandson! Who would do such a thing?

After turning the SUV around, she sped home. The shiny new bicycle she'd bought was staring at her from a corner of the living room. If it was only the bike, no problem. A grandmother could buy a bike for her grandson. But, no, she had to paint a bedroom blue and load it with boy stuff. Fill the closet with clothes for a six-year-old. She had to put a jungle gym and swing set in the back yard. Because she had gone overboard, the cops would suspect Guy had kidnapped his son, and they'd be on her doorstep any minute. They would figure he would hide him somewhere until the intense hunt subsided and then bring him home. What had she done?

There wasn't much she could do in the time she had, but she had to do *something*. The closet in her room was a large walk-in. Not the best solution, but better than nothing. She picked up the bike and hefted it up the narrow stairway, banging the wheels and handlebars against the wall, where they left black streaks.

Upstairs in her bedroom, shoes were scattered on the floor, underwear flung on the bed, and the stink of body odor hung in the air. In the closet, most of the hangers were empty, and clothes were piled on the floor. Aha! A perfect place to hide stuff—under the heap. She kicked garments aside, placed the bike flat on the floor, raced to the blue bedroom and scooped up as many toys as possible, then threw them on top of the bike. As she jumbled clothes on top, she heard the doorbell ring.

She felt her palms begin to sweat. Quickly, she finished concealing the bike and toys, and then hurried down the stairs. Through the glass panel in the door, she saw three men. One was in civilian clothes, and two were dressed in police uniforms, but she was confused. There was no squad car parked outside. Ah, an unmarked vehicle. She steeled herself and opened the door.

"Detective Madsen," said the man who held up a badge. Pointing to a tall man who appeared to be squinting, he said, "This is Officer Shepherd. And that's Officer Chen." The Asian man raised his hand in greeting.

"Got some questions to ask you. Can we come in?" Madsen stepped inside.

For once, she was glad of the moldy smell that filled her house. Perhaps it would drive them away. Madsen sat on the couch. Chen remained standing as did Shepherd, who took out a pad and pen. Madeline chose the armchair across the room, as far away as she could manage.

"Do you have any idea where your son might be?" Madsen leaned forward.

She knew they were watching her reaction, so she remained expressionless. "No."

"Have you made any attempt to contact Miss Jackie Ravinski in the last few weeks?"

"No."

Shepherd wrote something on his pad. "Why not? Wouldn't you want to see your grandson?"

"Jackie don't get along too good with me."

"When your son left prison, this is the address he gave, so he's been living with you. Where is Guy?"

Madeline felt perspiration break out on her forehead. "He did his time. Leave him be."

"Where is he?"

"Dunno."

"Do you mind if Officer Chen has a look around while we talk?"

She swallowed. She could say no, but then, they would just return with a warrant. She decided to get this over with. "Okay." Chen headed upstairs.

"Where was your son last night after seven o'clock?"

"Here."

"And you have someone who can confirm that?"

"Me." Shepherd was scribbling again. What the hell could he be writing?

"Did you visit your son while he was in prison?"

"Of course. Every week."

"I ask you again. Where can we find Guy?"

"Told you, dunno."

"Do you work?"

"At the Sunny Days nursing home. This week, I've been cooking dinner."

"Then how could you know whether your son was home last night or not?"

Looking down at her shoes, she didn't know how to respond, so she said nothing. She could hear the cop moving around upstairs.

"If we need to question you further, we can find you there tonight?"

"Suppose so."

"Good." Madsen was studying her. "Miss Ravinski ever visit your son in prison?"

No matter what she answered, they could check prison records. Probably already had. "Sometimes," she answered, still examining her shoes. From the sounds upstairs, she knew the cop was in the guest room. Overhead, the footsteps sounded as he moved into her room. She couldn't help herself; she looked up at the ceiling. Again, Shepherd noted something in that goddamned notebook.

Her right eye began twitching, and there was nothing she could do to stop it. She cleared her throat.

"Did Todd O'Malley ever come to talk with you?"

How did they know about that? She frowned and wiped her forehead with the back of her hand. "Maybe once or twice. Can't remember exactly how many times."

"What did you two talk about?" Madsen shifted his weight on the sofa.

Todd had wanted her to convince Guy to sell drugs in prison. Hell. He had come a lot more than twice. He'd been fucking frightening the last few times. "Nothing special." There were footsteps in the walk-in closet.

"You discussed your son."

"I never said that." Then it was quiet upstairs. What the hell was that cop doing in the closet?

Madsen's face was tight. He cleared his throat. "Exactly what deal did you make with Todd O'Malley?"

"Nothing." She realized her voice was too loud.

"Why did O'Malley visit your son on several occasions while he was locked up?"

That was news to her. Why hadn't Guy told her? At the same time she was wondering how to answer, she heard Officer Chen's footsteps on the stairs. At the same time, the door burst open and Guy charged in.

CHAPTER 18

At the police station, Zoey was pacing in the lobby. "Jackson responded quickly. I'm so glad."

"He knows his law. I've always been impressed with his work for the school." David placed his hands behind his head and interlocked his fingers. "How much is his fee?"

"Actually, I don't know. I didn't talk to him. Called him on my cell and left a message on his answering machine. Told him it was urgent." She paused and peered down the corridor. "What's taking so long? You don't think they're charging her do you?"

"I'll help with the fee."

"Oh, no need for that. But thanks."

"Well, the offer is there." He sniffed. "I doubt she'll be charged, but we'll know soon enough."

Finally, a door opened and Jackson Addison escorted Jackie into the lobby. Her shoulders were hunched and she was chewing on her lower lip. Her eyes were dazed. When she saw Zoey rushing toward her, she covered her face with her hands and sobbed. They embraced for a long time. When Zoey stepped back, the lawyer extended his arm. "Good to see you again, Zoey." She shook his hand. "She's free to leave. I'll be in touch with both of you." Zoey thanked him and he left.

David placed his hand on Zoey's shoulder. "I'm heading over to Ropewalk Court." He checked his watch. "It's almost two-thirty. According to Tom Madsen, a search ought to be starting over there. He's probably in the field already."

Zoey nodded and found herself alone with Jackie. "Have you eaten?"

She shook her head. "I couldn't possibly get anything down. I need to join that search."

"That's not a great idea. You look exhausted."

"I don't care. I'll go on my own if you won't take me."

"Okay, okay. You know I'll take you. We'll go search for Will together." They left the station, and Zoey helped her into the passenger seat of her car. As she pulled out of the parking lot, a car turned into the driveway with two uniformed officers in the front. She noticed Guy Falcone in the back seat. Since he was staring at the floor, and Jackie's eyes were closed as she leaned against the head rest, Zoey guessed they had not seen each other.

Guy wished Tom Madsen had come to the station with him instead of sending him with those two asshole cops. He had overheard Madsen say he was going to Ropewalk Court. While he sat alone in the dingy interview room, Guy heard the door open and that bastard Dalbeck walked in with a pad and pen. Noisily, he scraped a chair over and sat across the table. He clicked on a tape recorder, gave his name, Guy's name, the date, time, and purpose of the interview.

"Where were you last night after ten o'clock?"

"Home."

"And your mother will confirm that?"

"No one can. She was working."

"We have a witness who saw you outside Jackie Ravinski's house last night. What were you doing there?"

"That's impossible. I was nowhere near her home. "

"Tell me the truth. We know you took him. What have you done with Will?"

"Look, I came in here voluntarily. We both know I can walk out that door anytime I want."

"Real smart, ex-con. Knows how to beat the system." Dalbeck tapped the pen on the table. "You don't want to make this any harder on yourself. If you tell me how you kidnapped him, it will go easier on you."

"And I didn't ask for a lawyer 'cause I got nothing to hide."

"Explain what you and Jackie Ravinski talked about last night?"

"We didn't talk."

Dalbeck flexed his fingers, then cracked his knuckles. A woman with stringy hair and glasses came into the room with a clipboard and whispered in Dalbeck's ear. "Be right back," he said, and left the room with the woman. Guy pulled his chair forward, placed his elbow on the table and rested his chin in his palm. He made a decision. In a few minutes, the detective returned.

"I'm leaving now," Guy heard the weariness in his own voice. Dalbeck rolled up his sleeves and glared at him. Remaining immobile, the ex-con knew the detective had no choice but to let him go. When Dalbeck opened the door, he said, "This isn't over." Guy stood outside the police station and took a deep breath. The weather was decent enough, he decided. He would walk home.

CHAPTER 19

E arly afternoon! She always hated that time of day, never knew why, just always did. One, two, buckle my shoe. Tired of watching those shoppers rushing around, what a waste. So few kids shopping with their parents, and they're too old anyway, at least for her purposes. Too bad for her. Three, four, block the door.

That dim-witted security guard hid in that cube he called a room, with his eyes glued to those cameras, but she was too clever for him, always did her homework. She knew where each and every one of those cameras was located. Catch her? Ha! Never. Five, six, pick up sticks.

That damn migraine wouldn't quit, so she rolled down the window, leaned back against the head rest and closed her eyes, hoping for relief, but there was none. Somewhere a car engine sputtered and croaked and a man called out. The wind was strong and sharp like a burr stuck in a cat's fur. Seven, eight, don't be late.

Suddenly, just in time. A man, black coat collar turned up against the chill, hurried toward the store, holding his child's hand. She was dressed in a fluffy white jacket as she half-trotted in her little pink boots to keep pace with him, her auburn hair blowing in the wind. The perfect age. After zipping up the front of her polyester jacket, the woman pulled the drawstring in the hood so it encircled her face. She grabbed a canvas gym bag from the passenger seat and unzipped the top where a kid-sized Red Sox jacket hid the rest of the tools of her trade. That jacket would fit that girl just fine. She slipped on gloves and stepped onto the hard, cold pavement. Nine, ten, come to my den.

She tracked Little Miss Pink Boots into the store, from a safe distance, of course. Once inside, the girl wriggled to free herself from her father's hand, but his grip was firm. When she whined, he produced a tootsie roll from his pocket, bent down beside her and unwrapped the candy. When she took it from him, he smiled, lifted her up as she bit into the treat and held her so her face looked out over his shoulder, like the full moon. He continued down the aisle and stopped to inspect the gas grills.

The woman planted herself diagonally across from them so the father's back was to her. Little Miss Pink Boots was sucking her candy, peering over his shoulder, observing the few customers as they passed by, when an orange-vested salesman approached them. The woman's headache was aggravated by the glaring fluorescent lights. The girl, who by then had a chocolate circle for a mouth, stared directly at the woman, just as a stabbing pain skewered her brain. She pivoted away, dropped the bag and massaged her temples as she listened to the rustle and murmur of people passing behind her. In front of her was a display filled with hardware for kitchen cabinets: knobs, handles, latches, all gold and silver. Eleven, twelve, gold on the shelves.

"Are you all right?" a familiar voice asked. She turned. Damn! Blake was standing close to her in his Home Depot vest with concern etched into his face. "Oh, it's you," he said, "Feeling okay?"

She nodded. "One of my headaches."

He cricked his neck, left then right. "What're you doing here?"

She managed a smile, hoping it appeared genuine. "Picking something up."

A wrinkled man with a stubbly chin approached, wearing sweat pants and a purple jacket. He tapped Blake on his arm, sparing her further conversation. "Excuse me, fella. I need help with one of those alarms. I forget whatcha call them. You know, the kind that tells you there's a fire."

"A smoke alarm." said Blake.

"That's the one."

"I'll show you. Follow me."

"You gotta know when there's trouble in the house," the man said as they walked away.

The woman was pissed off—spotted, even worse, recognized. Reconciling herself to the abandonment of her project, she retrieved the gym bag and glanced back toward Little Miss Pink Boots, who was now standing beside her father. Bending over the open grill, he was listening intently to the salesman who was pointing out features.

Then it happened. The girl bolted from her father, darted by the woman and disappeared down aisle 34. The woman's response was impulsive and rapid. She hustled after the child. At the same time, she reached inside the satchel, her fingers finding the chloroform-drenched rag that she had loosely wrapped in plastic and hid beneath the Red Sox jacket. Lucky for her, no shoppers were in that aisle. She grabbed the girl by the shoulder, while simultaneously slapping the cloth over the child's face to muffle her cry. Immediately, she hauled her up and clutched the girl, so both her face and the rag were buried in the woman's shoulder. Sweat spontaneously dampened her palms. As she made a beeline for the bathroom, the girl struggled and kicked the bag dangling from her arm. Then Little Miss Pink Boots was still, moaning softly.

The woman kicked open the restroom door, banging it against a large trash can as she rushed in. Yes! They were alone. But what about Blake? Would he connect her with this missing child? Too late now.

Angrily she slammed open a stall door, which banged against the metal side and bounced shut again. "Focus," she said out loud to herself, "Hurry up." Inhaling deeply, she stepped inside the stall, locked the door, sat on the toilet seat and positioned Little Miss Pink Boots sidesaddle on her lap. When she removed the rag, the child groaned. After jamming the cloth into the bag, she checked her watch. Tick tock. Mind the clock. As she wrestled the girl's fluffy coat off, she heard the restroom door burst open. Had she been found out? Footsteps hurried into the stall next to hers.

Gray Nikes with orange shoelaces were inches from her bag. Hairs stiffened on the back of the woman's neck, but she was too far along; she couldn't turn back. A few folds of denim pantleg fell and covered the tops of the running shoes. Again, the girl started to groan, so the woman coughed repeatedly to hide the sound, while she crammed the child's arms into the sleeves of the Red Sox jacket, and snapped it shut over her sparkly sweater. Tick tock. Stop the clock.

Next she tugged at the pink boots, which slid off easily, and buried them in the tote. In the adjacent stall, water flushed, a lock clicked open and the gray shoes squeaked out of sight. Then, in her bag, she found black slacks and pulled them over the girl's tights printed with tiny pink hearts. Water splashed in a basin, a hand dryer whirred, then the bathroom door whooshed shut. The intruder was gone. She was safe.

When she tried to push on a sneaker with a Velcro strap, it was too small, so she squashed the girl's foot into it. The child whimpered. She shoved on the other shoe, stood, and sat the girl on the floor with her back against the toilet seat. Then for the scissors. Snip! Snip! Snip! Snip! She dumped the beautiful long locks into the toilet. Flush! The hair swirled, and then disappeared. Presto! The girl was a boy with an awful haircut. Tossed the scissors into the gym bag. Dug deep into the satchel and found the crown for Little Miss Pink Boots: a baseball cap with a red B. The woman placed it on the girl's head with the visor facing backwards.

After unloosening the drawstring under her own chin, the woman pulled at her hood and, with satisfaction, heard the snaps around the collar unfasten: bing, bing, bing. The hood separated from the jacket. Next, she reversed her jacket: black became the lining, sky blue the exterior. She tugged a tan knitted cap over her head, making sure all her hair was hidden. Then the woman held the girl so her face was buried in her shoulder, as if the child were sleeping. Checked her watch. Good! All accomplished in less than five minutes.

She unlatched the stall door. With her elbow, bumped the cover of the waste basket partially off its base—easy to do—shoved the gym bag inside, replaced the cover and walked out of the restroom.

Because she had investigated a few days ago, she knew that, just steps away behind the bathroom, a back exit was left unlocked. From the number of cigarette butts she had observed outside when she'd opened that door that day, the woman knew it was where employees went to smoke on their break. Within seconds, she was there. But when she turned the knob, the door didn't open. Probably stuck, so she rammed her shoulder into the door, but nothing happened. Locked! She panicked. The girl twisted in her arms. Tick tock. Damn that clock. The woman hoofed it down an aisle, which surprised her by ending a few feet from the customer service desk. She hadn't planned for that.

The wrinkled man was covering his mouth with his hands, his eyebrows raised in astonishment. His eyes were fixed on the girl's father, who was frantically waving his arms and shouting something at Blake, who was standing behind the counter, punching numbers into a phone. Her heart was thudding like a tom-tom. For a moment, she faltered as she watched Blake talking into the phone. Perhaps she could leave the girl behind, just dump her somewhere. Perhaps by that kitchen display, but she knew it was too late. A flicker of anxiety preceded her flash of anger. What the hell was wrong with me, she wondered. She was smarter than all of them. The man glanced at her, but she knew he only saw a napping boy dressed in a Red Sox jacket. Blake put down the cell phone and, mercifully, turned away from her.

As the woman averted her face and headed for the exit, she realized what a huge mistake Blake had made. He should have done the Code Adam before the phone call. She counted the steps to the exit…seven…eight…nine…ten. She was in front of the glass doors which began to slide open. All at once, the intercom screamed, "Code Adam, Code Adam, Code Adam." Where the hell had all those employees come from? Like bugs out of the woodwork, they were flying toward the doors.

"Hey, you! Stop!" a man yelled.

Some else called out, waving at her. "Halt! Right there!"

She was out the door, but the two employees were close behind and gaining. She heard their footsteps behind her. Every muscle in her body tensed as she raced across the parking lot to the van. Wind had intensified and whipped dried bits of leaves into miniature tornadoes.

In the distance, sirens wailed. The woman was at the van, sliding the back door open. Leaves danced inside. No time for the plastic zip ties. She threw the child on the back seat. The door glided shut as the woman jumped into the driver's seat and locked the doors. Her right hand was shaking so violently that she had to steady it with her left so she could get the key in the ignition. When the engine finally turned over, one of the employees was right outside, pounding on the glass. Damn! They had been fast! Accidently, she threw the van in reverse. When she floored the gas pedal, another employee, a teenager who was running behind the vehicle, had to dive to the asphalt to avoid being struck. As the woman jammed the van into first gear, she saw the teen rolling over in the parking lot. The man who had been pounding on the window was stumbling, trying to regain his footing. She headed out of the parking lot. Just before turning onto the main highway, cop cars streaked by, blue lights whirling, sirens screaming. She grinned. Tick tock. She beat the clock.

CHAPTER 20

Butch hurried down the stairs and into the passenger seat, reeking of Old Spice. Backing her Volkswagen out of Jackie's driveway, Becky noticed him gawking at her. Her jaw muscles tightened, and her shoulders curled forward.

He slipped a pack of Marlboros from his shirt pocket and tapped out a cigarette. "You know, Jackie wasn't much good at it."

"Not good at what?" She heard her own voice bristle.

Butch laughed. "Not what you're thinking."

She gripped the steering wheel. "You have no idea what I'm thinking. And I'd appreciate it if you didn't smoke in my car."

Mumbling something, he tucked the cigarette behind his ear. "Hey, don't be so touchy. I mean Jackie wasn't so hot at doing that mom thing."

"You don't know how good a mom she is or isn't. And I'm not being touchy."

"No money to speak of. Shit. That must be tough. No family. Boy's father's a jail bird. Now Will's gone. Just like that." He snapped his fingers. "He was a nice kid."

"Don't talk like it's all over for that child. And she has friends. Good ones. Better than some families."

"Nah. Blood's always thicker." He scratched his arm pit.

"Friends can be as thick." She turned onto Court Street.

"That lady school teacher comes around lots. I'll give you that." He sucked air through his teeth. "One hot momma. But that guy don't come round no more."

"What guy?"

"If he was family he'd be there for Jackie." Butch adjusted his pants around his crotch.

Becky ignored his action. "What guy are you talking about?"

"Curly hair. You know the one. Was with the school teacher all the time."

"You mean David? How do you know he's not there for her?"

"Cause I know stuff like that. Just like I know you got a thing for him."

"Are you out of your mind?"

"You were all over him last summer. You know, at the barbeque. Laughing and talking like there's no tomorrow. I saw you."

She couldn't believe it. This idiot was jealous. "What I was doing was being friendly."

"That kind of friendly leads to stuff." He whistled. "Like setting the bed on fire. Like we did."

"That was a mistake. Forget it."

"Those long legs of yours in mustard colored shorts. Can't forget that. Woman like you was made for loving."

Simultaneously, she wrenched the steering wheel to the right and stepped on the brake which jolted the front of the car over a curb and to a halt.

"Whoa! What're you doing?"

She glowered at him. "Listen to me! It was a mistake. It'll never happen again. Do you un-der-stand?" She emphasized each syllable.

"Sheesh! You don't have to half-kill us to make your point." He looked around and then jerked his head toward a nearby liquor store. "Wait 'til I get something?"

Without waiting for a response, he stepped from the car and swaggered toward the store. She slammed the car into park. "Hurry up!" But she knew he couldn't hear her.

Butch was a fool. How absurd he thought she was attracted to David. She thought about Zoey and David, how cute they looked as a couple, both short, he just a bit taller. She remembered a meal he had cooked for them in Zoey's apartment: salmon with a maple glaze. His cooking brought out a creative side, a playfulness. They had laughed a lot that night. Yet, at times, there was a restlessness about him, an anxiety he wasn't always able to hide.

She pictured David as a father, carrying a little girl on his shoulders, joking with a son. He yearned for that. Deep down, Zoey wanted a family too, but she was terrified of getting too close to a man. Even though Zoey had ended the relationship, she still loved him.

Butch emerged from the store, smoking his Marlboro and swigging from a can of Heineken. When he reached the car, he inhaled a long drag, then slowly exhaled before tossing the cigarette on the ground and grinding it out. Then he clicked open the door and slid in with his beer. Without a word, Becky pulled into traffic.

As soon as she had parked near Ropewalk Court, Butch bailed out of the car and headed toward the field where the search for Will had begun. Thank goodness I'm rid of him, she thought. The air was warm and humid for October and smelled heavy as lead. The sidewalk was slick, covered with leaves drenched by the storm. As she approached, she noticed an irregular line of people zigzagging through the field: police officers and volunteers, some carrying poles or knives, prodding and slashing at the tangle of undergrowth.

She spotted Zoey and Jackie, who had veered off from the throng and were headed for the remnants of what looked like a stone wall. It was hard to tell because the growth was so thick. It seemed unlikely that Will would be here, but he was only six. Maybe he had left Jackie's apartment on his own on some crazy adventure. Maybe he'd decided it would be fun to hide in this jungle. He could wriggle through this tangle better than any adult.

Becky followed the rough-hewn path Zoey had forged through the undergrowth, shouting for her friend.

CHAPTER 21

Zoey was hacking into a thick vine with an axe a volunteer had lent her, when she heard someone calling her name. Exhausted, she wrenched the blade from the wood, turned and spotted Becky trudging toward them. She was surprised at the intensity of the relief she felt at the sight of her buddy. Could any day be more horrible? Anxiety tugged at her about Jackie, who lagged behind her like a deflated balloon. What could possibly have happened? A smart kid, yes, but only six years old, and night would soon be upon them. She shivered involuntarily at the thought.

As Becky approached, a movement caught her attention. A figure was slogging toward David Roth and the two officers who were leading volunteers in a far section of the field. Just as Becky reached her, she realized who that person was. The frustration of the day poured out of Zoey. "Tell me you didn't bring Butch!"

Becky's eyebrows flew up and she jabbed her fists into her waist. "Such a greeting!"

Zoey didn't contain herself. She thumped the axe head onto the ground. "Not so long ago. How low did you feel? A one night stand with him."

"Are you saying another body looking for Will isn't helpful?"

"He couldn't have found another way of getting here?"

"You know damn well he doesn't have a car."

Zoey took a deep breath, trying to control her feelings. "I admire you in so many ways, but your judgment, well… it's not always the best. It will get you into trouble someday."

Becky leaned toward her. "I'll have you know…"

A moan grabbed their attention; Jackie had slumped to the ground, her face white and her eyes vacant. Immediately, both women knelt down next to her. Inwardly, Zoey chastised herself for not being more in touch with how affected Jackie had been by this horror of a day. She pulled her close and murmured soothing sounds, while Becky checked her pulse.

Jackie's voice was a puff of a whisper. "Don't… fight. I can't… It's all my fault. If I were a good mother, he'd be safe with me."

"That's not true." Becky stood up. "You need to rest. I'll take you home."

"I'm a horrible mother."

"Of course you're not." Zoey rocked Jackie as if she were a child. "This is all too much. It would be for anyone."

Vehemently, Jackie shook her head. "I can't leave. My baby…"

"You're not to blame."

"You're no good to anyone like this." Becky's voice was calm, but her face showed concern, and she picked at a fingernail. "Besides, you're slowing Zoey down."

Jackie gazed at Zoey, the unasked question in her eyes. Am I holding you back from finding my son? her eyes pleaded as clearly as if she had spoken aloud.

Zoey brushed Jackie's hair from her forehead. "Let Becky take you home." When Jackie looked away, she added, "Such a great job you've done with Will. He's a neat kid, and smart. He's not helpless. He'll need you at your best when we find him. You must rest, pull yourself together. The moment I know anything—"

"Promise?"

"Absolutely." Zoey helped her to her feet, and Becky squeezed her arm around Jackie's waist, as if holding her together.

"I feel as if I'm deserting him."

"We will find him." Her voice sounded more confident than she felt. Jackie surrendered to Becky, who exchanged a look with Zoey. Even with help from Becky, Jackie was struggling to get up, and Zoey realized how exhausted she must be. As she watched them retreat, she was gnawed by fear that Will might not be found. Then she turned away, squinted into the woods and focused again on her goal—the stone wall. The intuition that had washed over her when she first saw it reassured her now. That structure was significant. She retrieved the axe and resumed chopping a path. Sweat rolled off her body, and drops formed on the tip of her nose and fell to the ground. Every muscle in her body ached, and the axe felt heavier with each swing. Rotting vegetation released a sour odor into the air and into her lungs. Finally, close to tears, she let the axe thud on the ground, bent over and rested her hands on her thighs. Wondering where she would get the energy to continue, she realized she was almost there. She pushed branches aside and peered through the tangle of bushes. Fallen stones lay close to a section of intact wall.

She wiped damp hair from her forehead and resumed slashing at the vines until she reached a small clearing. Brush had been removed from an area by the wall. Odd, she thought. Being careful to disturb nothing, she stepped around the fallen stones and looked behind the wall. A large plywood board had been propped against the top, forming an impromptu lean-to. Vegetation had been ripped out from that ground also. Underneath the board, where the ground was protected from rain, she found a distinct boot print. Her heart pounded. Avoiding the print, she examined the remaining area and almost missed a tiny white object, partially buried in mud. If it's what she thought it was… She found David's number in her cell phone and tapped it.

CHAPTER 22

David Roth was surprised at the number showing on his caller ID. "Zoey, what's going on?"

"Will's been here. I've found something."

He could hear the excitement in her voice. "That's great, but Zoey, you could be in danger. What if someone is still in the area?" He could not bring himself to say "abductor;" it sounded too ominous.

"I don't think so. Doesn't look like anyone's here. Someone was, but not now."

"You don't know that for sure. Start back down the path you've made. I'll meet you. And hurry." He hung up.

"Any info?" That man who had arrived late was close to him, a vague smell of dirt drifting from his clothes. He had introduced himself as…what was it, Butch?

Annoyed and concerned about Zoey, David took a step back. "Light will be fading soon. Don't you think we all need to keep searching?"

"But anything new?" The man pointed to David's pocket. "Your phone call?"

"Nothing," David turned his back and took the few steps to where Detective Tom Madsen was standing, watching, with his arms crossed, sweat staining his shirt under his armpits. Keeping his voice low, David said, "Zoey's found something."

Butch had followed him; Madsen glared and stepped toward him. "Like he said, light will be fading." Then he pointed to a dead tree that had fallen against an oak, entangled with its branches. "Think you can cut your way to that tree by twilight?"

The man slid his eyes sideways and blinked. "Think so."

"Then do so." Madsen glanced back at David and jerked his head down the path.

Backtracking on the trail they had just cut, David briefly halted to make sure the stranger was not following. By the time he reached the juncture of Zoey's path, Madsen was trailing behind, but David did not wait for him to catch up.

Twilight was beginning to darken the afternoon sky, and neon light glowed on the horizon. For David, twilight brought loneliness; he was not sure why, and the darkening sky intensified his ache for Zoey. He loved her, wanted to marry her, have kids and spend the rest of his life with her.

The path she had hacked out was barely passable. But then, she was a small woman, he thought, feeling protective. He admired her; her size never prevented her from tackling difficult situations, and her wits and tenacity overcame problems—most of the time anyway.

As he followed the trail, he thought about Zoey's suspension from her job and anger stirred him. David believed the new principal was the wrong choice for the job. Either a mistake had been made or politics had been at play.

At the Annie Sullivan Charter School, everyone wore many hats. "Guidance counselor" was his official title, but he had helped restrain out-of-control teens, broken up fights and pursued kids who'd fled the building. Last week, arriving early at school, he had comforted a student he found wearing socks but no shoes, curled up asleep by the front door of the school because he had fled violence in his own home. They had eaten bagels and drank juice as the teen shared his trauma of the night before.

But Peter Kroger believed in rigid roles; staff should perform only the duties they were hired to do, no more, no less. And he believed in punishment, of the old-fashioned spare the rod and spoil the child variety. However, that thinking did not work in an alternative school. Their students had multiple and diverse needs. Staff needed to be flexible. And empathy and compassion were essential; life had punished these students enough.

David knew where the principal stood on women's issues; if Zoey were a man, he would have treated her differently. She would have had a good talking to and the problem would never have gone to the Board. Worst of all, David suspected that Peter Kroger wasn't a straight shooter.

Something skittered in the bushes and he swiveled in that direction. Branches were trembling and he heard something growl. He hustled sideways, and in doing so, scratched himself on a ragged branch, tripped over a root humping from the ground, fell and ripped a hole in the knee of his trousers. Fortunately, whatever animal it was had retreated. After rolling over, he sat up and examined the tear in his slacks and the damage to his throbbing knee. A few scratches. In a day, a purple bruise would blossom, but nothing serious. He pushed himself up and continued on the path.

Why hadn't they met up by now? Where the hell was she? He was about to call her on his cell phone when he saw someone moving about through the bushes up ahead. With his next step, branches cracked beneath his foot and a person called out, "David?"

"Yup." He continued pushing aside branches for a hundred yards and stepped into a small clearing surrounded by a tangle of vines and bushes. "Why didn't you come down the path?" He found a stick and probed the surrounding brush, peering into the woods until he was satisfied no one was there. He tossed the stick into the woods, and then stood close to her, noticing passion flit across her eyes. His annoyance faded; he pulled her to him and kissed her. She leaned into him. "I miss you horribly," he said, and breathed in her sweetness.

He felt her weight against his chest, but then she pushed away. Suddenly, she was all business and stepped over a pile of debris to a place near the lean-to. Pointing to an object in the mud, she said, "I made that for him." Her voice was husky.

The sky had darkened. Although he saw what she was pointing at, he pulled his keychain from his pocket, squatted down, and shined his penlight on it. In the mud, small dark stones glinted between white miniature blocks that were connected by chain links. Each block was imprinted with a letter. They spelled W-I-L-L.

"He must have gotten it off somehow. I'm sure he dropped it here for us to find," she said.

Thinking there might be another explanation, David studied the scene. "What a strange place to bring a kid. Why not an apartment or a house? And how in the world did anyone get in here? The brush is so thick."

"Don't you see? The clasp isn't broken. He left it on purpose."

"However it got in the mud, we know he was here." He stood up. "Can't a jewelry clasp accidentally come open?"

"Not mine. I buy the best." She pointed to the right. "It looks like there's a trail over there. It's all overgrown, but someone could have come in that way. I think it leads to an old building that was part of the rope factory."

Slowly, he played the light down the trail, over the plywood lean-to, the wall and mud, until it rested on a boot print.

"If I'm not mistaken," Zoey said, "that's a cowboy boot. In my teens, I was the proud owner of a pair. The toe is narrow and squared off. Notice how smooth the sole is. Lots of cowboy boots don't have any tread."

He examined the print closely. "You might be right. But it could be the mud didn't register any marks. Madsen will know what to do when he gets here." He directed the light under the plywood. A tarp covered the ground. An empty soda bottle and a torn bag with POPCORN in bright orange letters lay on top. A plastic bag held crusts of bread.

"Whoever was here left in a hurry." She sighed. "I'm glad he wasn't in this place for too long."

He heard someone coming, and a light crisscrossed through the branches. Madsen stepped into the clearing, panting. Sweat stained his shirt. "Crap-ass bushes." He rubbed at scratches. Zoey and David shared their observations with him, and pointed to the trail that led to the old rope factory building.

"Listen, guys," Zoey said, "Monica and Kurt are looking into Will's disappearance too. I don't know what they've found, if anything, but I'm meeting them at their house. You know, compare notes and figure out what else we can do. Over Chinese takeout." She checked her watch. "I'll be heading over at six."

"Aren't they journalists?" Madsen asked. He turned to his friend. "I remember you mentioning them on occasion."

"They publish an online magazine, *Front and Center*."

"Yeah. That was it."

"How about you two coming over, sharing notes and having some Chinese?" Zoey suggested.

"Thanks, but I can't." Madsen said. "To start with, this scene needs to be secured. I'm assuming you two know better than to mess with anything."

"Of course," David answered. To Zoey, he added, "I'll meet you over there." Then he placed his hand on Zoey's back and shined the penlight at the path. "Stay close."

Zoey picked up the axe and followed him down the path toward her car.

CHAPTER 23

Lots of changes, thought Monica as she drove her Lexus through Quincy Center. How many years since her father had brought her and Zoey here to see the history?

A light turned red and Monica stopped. Directly across the street stood the First Parish Church where John Hancock's father had served as pastor. Below street level, the church embraced a Presidential Crypt where John Adams and his son were entombed with their wives. She felt a tug of sadness, as she remembered listening to the tour guide while her father held her hand.

She sighed. Those online subscriptions to newspaper archives usually gave her something, but this time they had yielded nothing. What a waste of money! Frustrated by the results of her research, Monica drummed her fingers on the steering wheel as she waited for the light to change. Patience, she reminded herself. She knew not all microfiche stashed in libraries had been converted into internet files. Not yet anyway.

Patience not being one of her virtues, when her research had turned up nothing, she had slammed her laptop shut and had gone to the microfiche section in the Plymouth library. Grumbling to herself, she had found a box dated May, 1994–November, 1994. After inserting film into a machine, she had scrolled past headlines and ads, and paused at a mug shot of O.J. Simpson. Was that really twenty years ago? Not only had O.J.'s life changed that summer, but the axis of her own world had shifted forever. Suppressed memories began to push their way into her consciousness, but she had been able to stuff them back down and block the pain that inevitably accompanied them. Busying herself in the archives, she had found what she was looking for.

A horn beeped behind her, and she saw the light was finally green. As she pulled into a parking spot, she realized her hands were trembling and she felt weak. She had been feeling irritable for a while, but, foolishly, she had been ignoring the symptoms. Damn diabetes! She retrieved a pint-sized carton of orange juice from her handbag and gulped it down. Leaning back, she closed her eyes to rest and let the juice do its work.

She'd found the incident that had taken place twenty years ago. In the defunct *Plymouth Journal*, dated June of 1994, a headline had popped out: "Quincy Woman Sells Stolen Babies." The article had been short: "Yesterday, police arrested Krista Kappel, 34, of 1054 Beach Street, for selling infants that she abducted. The price for the children was presented as fees for the Right Adoption Agency. The unsuspecting couples were hoping to adopt white infants. Kappel will be arraigned in court on Monday."

That Krista Kappel, what a scum bag! Taking advantage of couples who desperately wanted children. But something nagged at her. There was more to the story of stolen babies, but she wasn't able to remember what. But she suspected it was important, so here she was in Quincy, headed for the library to search for more information in the local paper.

She began to feel better. Had her irritability resulted from low blood sugar, or from resurrected family memories jogged loose by the mug shot of O.J. Simpson? About the same time the police had chased O.J.'s white Ford Bronco down a Los Angeles freeway, Monica's father had closed the front door of their home for the last time. She opened her eyes and shook her head to exorcize the memory. The orange juice had worked its magic. She felt steady and her strength was mostly back. Dinner and Zoey! She had forgotten. After yanking her phone from her bag, she called her husband. When he answered, she asked, "Any word on Will yet?"

"No." She heard the sadness and tension in his voice.

"Zoey there?"

"No, it's early yet."

"I'm in Quincy, still researching. I'm running late."

"Figured you would be, so I... "

Feeling criticized, her response was automatic, rapid-fire. "Hey! I'm onto something important. Don't worry. I'll still get dinner."

"Dear, please stop. I was trying to say, I saved you the trouble. I already picked it up."

"Oh!" Monica felt apologetic and loved at the same time. Would she ever get over her distrust of men?

"Bought some Thai favorites of yours instead of Chinese: basil fried rice, tamarind duck, pad Thai, stir-fried vegetables." She imagined him grinning, pleased with himself, and she smiled at the thought.

"Yum! You're my hero. Love you. Gotta go." She clicked off and climbed out of her car with her laptop and handbag, then sprinted into the library where she found rows of boxes filled with microfiche. She selected two and skimmed articles until she reached June 17, where she read:

"Woman Arraigned in Baby Plot. Krista Kappel pled not guilty to five felony counts of child abduction and six counts of child trafficking. Allegedly, she snatched infants and masqueraded as a social worker representing an adoption agency. 'I left my baby for one second on the porch,' said Pamela Brunk. 'When I went inside to answer the phone, it turned out to be a wrong number. This is a nightmare. Whoever took my baby, please bring her back.'

"Police took a computer and several boxes of documents from the home of the accused. Kappel refuses to cooperate. Late this afternoon, she was released on bail."

Monica gasped at the next two lines of the article. "She allegedly sold her own six-year-old son. The whereabouts of her daughter is still unknown."

How could a mother sell her own child? Had she sold her daughter too? If not, what happened to her? Monica placed her hand on her abdomen. She and Kurt had tried so hard to have a baby, and finally, she had become pregnant! Since she was diabetic, the baby was at risk, which caused her to worry incessantly. She had tested her blood sugar forty times a day. Although her doctor had not ordered total rest, she had spent most of the day in bed. Kurt had been wonderful, doubling his work load by taking on housework, grocery shopping and preparing dinners.

Then, one day, during a routine exam, as she lay flat on a hospital table with Kurt holding her hand, an ultrasound technician had guided a transducer over her abdomen. Indefinite lines pulsed on the screen, then became clear. There he was, floating, connected to her umbilical cord. His mouth had moved in and out as he sucked his thumb! She had heard his heart beating. Kurt had cleared his throat and said, "Our son, Thomas."

She had miscarried. Her body had taken a long time to recover, but she needed to try again, as soon as possible. Kurt thought she was irrational, denying the danger of her diabetes. He worried that he would lose her with another pregnancy. She would be all right, she had promised, but he had insisted they adopt. She'd refused.

In the library, Monica tried to ignore her feelings as she printed out the article on the theft of children and threaded the next microfiche. What had happened to Krista Kappel and the children she sold? And her missing daughter?

On her way home, Monica suddenly remembered where the idea of a connection between Will's disappearance and the selling of children had come from. In the garage, that's where it would be. She would check in the place where she and Kurt stored the overflow of boxes from their basement. Soon, they'd have to sort through them and decide what to keep—or they'd be parking their cars on the street.

When she returned home, Zoey and David's cars were outside. Hmmm. Perhaps something romantic was sparking between them again. Deep down, she hoped so. Underneath the tangle of sibling crap, she knew her connection with Zoey was strong. Just took a lot of digging to find it.

The garage door rolled up, and she drove her Lexus in, parking next to Kurt's BMW. Not all the boxes were labeled, nor were they in any particular order. She selected one at random. Kurt's stuff: yearbooks, sweatshirt from William and Mary, campaign pin for Bill Clinton. Closing the flaps, she put it back in its slot. This might take a while.

Ten boxes, and stacks of memorabilia later, she found what she was looking for. Mixed in with a dried prom corsage, her senior class picture—my, how young she looked—a tennis racket and tickets from a Bob Dylan concert at Boston Garden. That one stopped her, a gift from her father. Holding those tickets in her hand didn't bring back sadness; she felt his love again. That concert had been in January, five months before he left. She shuffled through the rest of the contents until she found what she'd been looking for.

CHAPTER 24

Zoey placed flatware on the kitchen island and serving spoons into bowls of steaming food, while her brother-in-law, Kurt, answered the knock on his front door. When she heard David's voice, she bit her lip hard, as if that would stop the stirrings she felt, and then wondered if she should have invited him after all. His laughter in the hallway reminded her of the fun they had together, but it also brought regret. She wished she hadn't opened up to him in that field, because she didn't want to hurt him again. And she knew her fear of intimacy was greater than her desire to be close to him.

When he said her name, she heard huskiness in his voice as she fixed a smile on her face before turning to greet him. Dark circles puffed under his eyes and his shoulders slumped. She wanted to comfort him, but instead, she removed plates from the cupboard and set them next to the food, then fussed with the napkins. Kurt opened a bottle of cabernet sauvignon, invited them to sit, and they chose stools opposite each other at the island.

"Where's Monica?" asked Zoey, trying to ignore how close David's hand was.

"Running late." Kurt poured wine into a glass and offered it to him. "Good to see you again, my friend. Like old times."

"Thanks." David leaned toward Zoey and slipped his hand over hers. "Say, who's that character that Becky brought today?"

She felt tingling in her palms. Leaving her hand where it was, she avoided his eyes, stealing a glimpse of him only once. "Name's Butch Crow. He calls himself The Balloon Man. Real scum ball. Works off and on at Teddy Bear Day Care doing odd jobs. Sometimes, during tourist season, he makes balloon animals for kids down near the Mayflower. Does it in Fanueil Hall too. He doesn't get paid, just makes tips." She felt David's gaze on her, so she removed her hand and started to tap her foot. "It bothers me that he's around kids so much."

"Out in the field, he wasn't very helpful." David reached for a plate, spooned on rice and topped it with duck. "He found a stick and poked at some bushes where it was obvious there was nothing to find. Asked way too many questions. What's his connection to Becky, anyway?"

"Just a bad memory." She looked up at him. "Jackie told me there's no evidence of a break-in or struggle at her apartment." She made a clucking sound. "You know, she leaves that spare key under a flower pot. Might as well leave the damn thing in the lock."

Kurt piled food on his own plate and sat down next to her. "So if Jackie had nothing to do with Will's disappearance, he must have known the person who took him."

"Possibly. He's a heavy sleeper, though. A bomb wouldn't wake him."

"I saw that Will's photo and info's been posted on Missing and Exploited Children," Kurt said.

"Great." David took a forkful of duck. "In the field, Madsen told me that helicopters were searching. Cops from several towns were involved, and sex offenders were being questioned."

Zoey shifted her weight on her stool. "Did you guys know that Jackie broke up with Blake?"

"What's he like?" Kurt asked. "Would he get back at her by harming Will?"

She shrugged. "Dunno."

David waved his fork in the air. "Guy Falcone's out of prison and Will's his kid. Maybe he took him."

Kurt turned to him. "If I remember correctly, wasn't he was arrested for selling cocaine?"

"Yup. Tom was none too pleased at his release. Said he got out because he was a model prisoner and told the parole board he'd learned his lesson. Apparently he convinced them that the only reason he distributed drugs was to get money for Jackie and his boy."

"And your friend, Madsen, thinks that's a load of crap."

"Sure does. Guy is living with his mother, and, from what Tom says, she's over-the-top protective of him."

"It's understandable. She is his mother." Kurt speared a piece of duck.

David scratched his head. "The point I'm trying to make is, Guy's mother doesn't think things through; she reacts emotionally and way too strong to events."

"I believe Guy," Zoey said. "About why he sold drugs. I know he was crazy in love with Jackie. Might still be. He'd do anything for her."

Kurt asked David, "Are you saying Guy's mother may have taken Will?"

"Maybe."

Zoey cocked her head. "Did I just hear your garage door?"

Kurt slid off his seat and began preparing a plate for Monica. "Before you came in, Zoey was telling me that Will was held in that field."

"Yup. Hey, Zoey, you veered off the main search and found that lean-to." David's expression was full of admiration. "How'd you know to do that?"

"Some vegetation looked odd, broken where it shouldn't have been."

"But there's lots of fallen branches in there."

"Intuition." She raised her eyebrows and put her hand on her abdomen. "Felt it right here, in my gut." She laughed. "Maybe because I'm short, my perspective is different than yours."

"You're not much shorter than me." David smiled at her. "I think you're right about the print. Being a cowboy boot, I mean." To Kurt he said, "Nearly a perfect imprint in the mud, which was lucky, considering that downpour."

The front door slammed and Monica swooped in. As she greeted everyone, she plunked her laptop and purse on the floor and swung onto a stool. As Kurt caught his wife up to their conversation, he zapped the plate he had filled for her in the microwave and placed the steaming food in front of her. "How'd your research go?"

She slapped the table. "I found that old story."

"How so?"

"In the library, I found a newspaper article about this woman, named Krista Kappel, who was arrested for selling babies. She rented an apartment in the Wollaston Beach area in Quincy."

Zoey was curious. "Quincy? The beach?" She leaned forward. "What was the address in Wollaston?"

Monica stretched out her legs and kicked off her boots. She chuckled. "Beach Street. Appropriate, isn't it? But let me finish the story. "

"Do you remember the number?"

"Of course I do." Monica frowned and turned so her remarks were directed to the two men. "Well, it looks like this Kappel woman sold five babies, then she sold her own toddler son. That bitch. Can you believe that?"

Zoey placed her hand on her sister's shoulder. "What was it?"

"What? Oh, the house number? Honestly, can't you wait until I finish?" Monica wiggled her toes. "Ten fifty four. Krista Kappel rented an apartment in the Wollaston Beach area in Quincy."

"Then they were neighbors."

"Who?"

"Becky's grandmother."

"I thought she lived at nine hundred something."

"Well, almost a neighbor, down the street a little way. The point is, Becky's grandmother was the social butterfly of Wollaston Beach. She might have known her."

"Anyway, Krista Kappel's daughter disappeared at the same time those babies were sold."

"So when she was arrested, the daughter was already gone," Kurt said.

"Right, my love. When she made bail, she skipped out on the trial. No one has seen that monster since." She massaged her foot. "I know it's a long shot, but maybe she has reappeared and is selling children again. Maybe Will is one of them."

"How did you finally remember that the story from twenty years ago was all about this woman selling children?" Kurt asked.

Monica reached into her pocketbook and pulled out the newspaper she had found in the garage. Looking pleased with herself, she turned to the page she wanted, and then handed it to her sister.

The paper smelled musty. "How old is this?" Zoey asked. "Why do you have this—" she held it up between her thumb and index finger " —paper?"

"Turn to page seven."

The newspaper crinkled as she turned pages which smelled like a damp basement. "Oh," she laughed, "I remember now. That's the article you wrote in that summer journalism class when you were in high school." She showed David and Kurt the article. The headline read, *Summer Storyteller Series Begins at Crane Library.*

"My first published article."

"I'd like to read it." Kurt was smiling as he looked over Zoey's shoulder.

Monica stopped massaging her foot and spoke to her husband. "I had an assignment to write an article of my choosing. That summer we spent a lot of time with Becky's grandmother. At least Zoey did. Maggie Armstrong introduced me to a friend of hers who worked in the library in the children's room. Laura Snow, I'll never forget that name. She gave me the information, and *The Quincy Banner* was happy to print it."

"You even got a byline." Kurt laughed.

"Now look at the first page."

Zoey turned to the front page, glanced at the headline, then looked at Monica, "Your story was in this paper, the same day the article appeared about the Kappel crime."

"That's why this felt familiar to you," Kurt said.

"Look, the reporter included a copy of the ad this Kappel woman had originally placed in the newspaper." Zoey read the title of the advertisement out loud. "Right Adoption Agency. As she scanned the ad, her eyes widened. "Ohmygod! This layout looks exactly like the one on the internet. In fact, some of the phrases are the same."

Monica snatched the paper back and stared at the ad.

Zoey reached over and pointed. "Look. This adoption ad refers to an 'affiliation' with Smith College." She added, "Just like the internet ad mentioned an 'affiliation' with Harvard University."

Monica stared at her sister. "You may be right, but it might just be a coincidence."

Zoey took the paper back and examined the ad again. "I don't think so." She added, "If I'm not mistaken, both of them mention three boys and three girls. Do you still have that DNA ad?"

"Sure do," Monica hurried to retrieve the ad from her desk and handed it to Zoey, who checked the internet printout. She held them adjacent to each other. "Both schemes in these ads deal with something unique." Zoey's voice was excited. "Because of legalized abortion, not many white babies were available for adoption at that time. And that's exactly what this product was all those years ago."

"Choosing a trait for a child by manipulating the DNA is also a unique product," Monica added.

"A rare one," Kurt said, "and both deceptions have to do with children."

"Even if the same person wrote both ads, we don't know if any of this is connected to Will," David said.

"You're right," Zoey agreed, "but it's worth taking a closer look."

"Any chance it might be someone copying what that Kappel woman did?" David asked.

Monica replied, "Who would know about an ad like that from an obscure little paper called *The Quincy Banner?*"

"I'm impressed. You two woman are something else." David stood up and rubbed his stomach. "That was delicious. Thanks for dinner. I hate to eat and run, but I want to find out more about that Butch Crow character. He might be tied up in all this somehow."

"How long has Will been missing now?" Zoey asked.

David checked his watch and frowned. "A little over thirteen hours." Then he surprised everyone by lifting her chin and kissing her. He raised his hand in parting.

After he left, Monica slapped the counter again. "How about that!"

"Where do we go from here?" Kurt asked.

CHAPTER 25

"You're going to collapse if you keep pacing like that." Becky sat at the kitchen table in Jackie's apartment, tapping her fingers. Stopping at the open door to Will's bedroom, Jackie stared at his unmade bed and then slouched back through the living room, only to return to the bedroom.

"You're on pure adrenaline. You need to rest." Becky picked her pocketbook up from the floor and removed a vial of Xanax. "A tranquilizer would help."

Jackie's eyes darted at her, then away, as she continued pacing.

Becky placed her hand at the base of her neck and drew in a deep breath. For a long moment, she remained immobile. Then she stood, went to the stove, turned the burner on under the kettle and placed two mugs from the cupboard on the counter. Dropped two Xanax into a cup, crushed it with a spoon. Before placing teabags into the cups, she smothered the pill with honey. When the kettle whistled, she poured boiling water, sputtering into the mugs. Becky stirred the liquid until the bits dissolved.

When the tea had brewed, she held up the mugs, "Join me." Jackie hesitated, so she said, "Do it for me. I'll feel better if you have something in your stomach."

Jackie sighed, slumped at the table, and blew on the tea. "What if they don't find him?"

"I'm sure they will. You said nothing was disturbed, so I'm sure he wasn't harmed." She was relieved when Jackie started to drink the tea.

After the tranquilizer took effect, and Jackie was settled into the futon in the living room, Becky relaxed into an armchair. Jackie's apartment was sparsely furnished, but it was cheerful: the futon and armchair were a canary yellow, and a flowered throw rug nestled under a wooden coffee table with two of Will's books, *Superheroes*, and *Sharks*. Across the room, a television sat on a wooden plank held up by concrete blocks that had been painted lavender.

Startled by the doorbell, Becky peeked out a window and cringed when she saw who it was. Straightening her shoulders, she stepped onto the porch, and quietly closed the door behind her. "What're you doing here?"

Dara Lee was chewing gum, none too pleased to see who was minding the store. "What's going on?"

"She's resting."

"Well, I wanted to talk to her." Dara Lee thrust out a hip aggressively and propped her fists on her waist.

"Can't it wait?" Becky sat in one of the plastic chairs near the door. She did not invite the woman to join her.

Dara Lee strutted across the porch and perched on the railing. "Has Guy been by to see her yet?"

"Now, why should he come around here?"

"He's Will's father."

"So."

"So, they should be a family."

"Jackie's a lot better off without Guy Falcone in her life."

Dara Lee cracked her gum and then spit it over the railing. "That's just your opinion."

"Isn't there something useful you could be doing? Like helping to find Will instead of running around trying to play matchmaker?"

Dara Lee's face contorted with rage, and Becky wondered if that kind of anger could have driven her to harm the boy. But what would be her motive? However, this focus on reconciling Jackie and Guy, instead of helping to find Will, would make sense if Dara Lee already knew his whereabouts.

"Guy is a better choice for Jackie." Dara Lee pulled a pack of gum from her pocket, unwrapped another piece and stuffed it into her mouth. She plopped the pack into her pocket without offering a piece to Becky. "She was smart to break it off with Blake."

"Ah, I see. You do know that the whole world knows you'd love to have Blake in your hip pocket."

"You know nothing." Dara Lee's eyes narrowed into slits, and Becky felt a shadow of fear pass through her. "And what about David Roth? The whole world knows you'd love to get him in your pants."

Becky laughed. "Don't project your desires on me." She slapped her thighs, stood up and smiled. "How about this? I'll give you a call when she wakes up."

Dara Lee studied Becky for a long moment. She looked like she was about to say something else when she slithered from the railing; her eyes darted between Becky and the door. "Be sure to do that," she said and clunked down the steps in her platform shoes.

Later, when she checked on Jackie, she found she had rolled over on the futon and was moaning in her sleep. Becky removed a throw cover from the back of a chair, placed it over the girl and snuggled the edges under her body.

CHAPTER 26

Leaving Monica's house after dinner, Zoey was remembering David's kiss, his mouth on hers, when her cell phone rang. She dug it from her purse and checked the caller ID. Damn! Principal Kroger. She clicked it on. "Hello."

"Zoey, you have no business prancing around some field in public view during school hours. You do know you are still employed at Annie Sullivan."

How dare he?! "I am on leave. If you remember correctly, it is *unpaid.*"

"Doesn't matter. Questions could be raised. I want you in my office first thing in the morning."

"Why?" But he had already gone. She threw her phone into her pocketbook. He was finding any excuse to harass her. The man was a jerk. And how had known she was in the field during school hours? Probably some uptight parent.

But her thoughts didn't linger on the principal. She checked the clock on the dashboard. Just after seven-thirty. She smiled. Lots of elderly folks would be tucked in for the night, but not Becky's grandmother. Perhaps it was time to talk to her. Zoey punched 411 into her cell phone and asked for Maggie Armstrong's number.

After hearing Zoey's explanation of the events, Becky's grandmother insisted she drive to Quincy that night because she had information as well as a few photos that might be helpful.

When Zoey arrived at Maggie's house, the porch light was glowing. Maggie answered the door bell wearing a short-sleeved yellow nightgown with a cartoon of Minnie Mouse on the front. Her blue eyes were intelligent and her white hair was short and neatly curled. Bobbing up and down, a parakeet perched on her shoulder as Maggie leaned on her cane.

"How wonderful to see you. Next time Becky and I go to Foxwoods, you'll have to play hooky. You know, work isn't all it's cracked up to be."

Zoey laughed. Little did she know.

With mugs of hot tea and a plate of cheesecake brownies waiting on the coffee table, they nestled into the sofa, and Maggie told Zoey what she knew about Krista Kappel.

"On summer mornings, before my knee went bad on me, I used to take long walks in the neighborhood and chat with folks. She'd always be sitting on the front porch, and I'd wave to her, but she wouldn't acknowledge my presence. Her babies were always in a play pen. I had the impression she pretty much ignored them."

"Is that the boy she sold and the girl that went missing?"

Maggie pressed her lips together and her eyes had a distant gaze. "Yes." Then she sipped her tea and cupped the mug with her hands. "You probably saw them when I took you and Becky to Wollaston Beach, but they were only toddlers then. All the neighbors would get together and chat while we kept an eye on the children. Krista never joined in—always kept to herself."

Zoey chose a brownie, bit into it and savored its chocolate gooiness.

"I felt sorry for her, she seemed so isolated. That's why I never gave up trying to strike up a friendship. I'd stop and talk about the weather or some nonsense, even though she rarely responded. Once in a while, I baked some goody for her."

"If it was like this, I'm sure you made an impression on her." She took another bite and smacked her lips.

Maggie laughed and looked pleased. "Anyway, finally she warmed up a bit. Asked me to sit on the porch with her. She grew to trust me, probably as much as she trusted anyone."

"What was she like?"

"A bit unbalanced, I'd say. And bitter. Her husband had been wealthy. Bought a large parcel of land and built their dream home. Said she was happy living in Pepperell when the tragedy struck. That's how she put it – the tragedy. Her husband was killed. Her explanation for his death was…well…vague. Perhaps she didn't want to tell me. But she made him out to be a perfect human being."

"Did you have the sense she was being honest with you?"

"Oh, I believe her story was real enough." Maggie removed the top of a glass jar on the coffee table and chose an oatmeal treat which she offered to the parakeet. He nibbled at it fastidiously. "Her husband's death threw her into a tailspin, in every way. She said she was financially ruined. Couldn't bear living in their mansion, although the insurance money paid off the mortgage."

Zoey's eyes opened wide. "Doesn't sound like a financial disaster to me."

"Depends what you're used to."

"How'd she end up in Quincy?"

"She said a cousin lived here, although I never saw anyone visit. She rented the first floor apartment. A small place, especially with two babies." The parakeet chirped, took the treat and flew onto a nearby lamp. "Before I forget—" Maggie reached for an envelope on the table and gave it to Zoey. "Here are the pictures I told you about. Krista and her toddlers."

Zoey pulled them out and glanced at them, "Lovely woman." She tucked the photos into her pocketbook. "What happened to the house in Pepperell?"

"I don't think she ever sold it."

CHAPTER 27

After dinner, David Roth left Kurt and Monica's house, unconsciously smiling, encouraged by Zoey's warmth. Perhaps they'd be together again soon. As soon as he dug his keys from his pocket and climbed into his Hyundai, his thoughts turned to Butch Crow. David figured he might be connected to Will's disappearance. Somehow, he planned on talking with him.

As he approached Crow's apartment, he spotted him turning the corner at Burial Hill, so David pulled over to the curb and watched him stroll toward the waterfront, swinging a six pack of beer and whistling. When a young woman passed him, he turned his head. He must have commented, because she held her hand over her head and projected her middle finger.

After parking his car at a meter, David slipped a few quarters into the slot and followed him. Crow chose a bench across from Isaac's, overlooking Plymouth harbor. Several boats were calmly bobbing in the water. He plunked down the beer and sat. David waited until he popped open a can and settled in. Slowly walking by, he stopped in front of Crow. "Oh, hey, weren't you at the search today?"

"Yeah, I remember you." Butch's eyes narrowed. "Weren't none too friendly."

"Sorry. Don't take it personally." David held his palms up in the air. "I was concerned about the boy. Concentrating on that. But I do apologize."

Butch slugged down beer.

"It was good of you to help." He waited a few seconds before continuing, letting the compliment sink in. Crow probably didn't get many of those. "I heard about the search on the news, so I figured I'd join in."

"Yeah. That kid lives downstairs from me with his momma."

"I'd hate having a child live so close to me. All that noise."

"He's better now that he's older. An okay kid, really. Sometimes he's out in the backyard by himself. Don't see any friends around. He must be kinda lonely. I'll go down. Play catch with him."

David realized this man actually cared about Will.

Crow coughed and spit on the ground. "In summer, his momma lies on a blanket in that bikini of hers." Slowly he shook his head. "Hmmm….She's one foxy lady. You know what I mean." He swigged his beer and twisted his head to look up at David. "Take a load off." He moved over on the bench. "I'm Butch Crow." They shook hands.

"David Roth."

"Want a beer?"

"Sure, thanks." He sat, took the Budweiser, and opened the can. It was cold, and he enjoyed the taste and the feel of fizz on his tongue. "I don't feel like going to work tomorrow," David said, hoping Crow would talk about his job, but the silence stretched on between them. "You look like you have a tan." he added. "Are you lucky enough to work outside?"

"Used to. Then I injured my back. Got on disability. I've been able to milk that one for a long time." He laughed. "Dumb-ass bleeding heart bureaucrats."

David laughed too, hoping Crow would take it for agreement.

"I make balloon animals for tips. It's kinda fun. The kids like it." He held up his Budweiser. "Keeps me in beer. Cheers." They clinked their cans together. "Speaking of dumb-ass people, last Memorial Day, I bought a grill at one of those, you know, big box stores. Used it the whole week-end. I returned it the following Tuesday and got my money back. Told them it didn't work right. They just took my word for it. I didn't even clean it. Brought it back with meat still stuck on the grill."

"They didn't even try to see if it worked or not?"

"Nope. Like I said, dumb-ass."

David wondered how far Butch Crow would bend the rules. "Not to change the subject, but how well do you know your downstairs neighbor?"

"Not so much. Her name's Jackie. She always invites me to her annual barbeque. Had a steady boyfriend for a few years, but they must have broke up. When I didn't see him coming around, I asked her out, but I guess I'm not her type. She was real polite about saying no, So I left her alone."

David was surprised. From what he had heard, this man was a lecher, but Butch Crow could treat a woman with respect.

"Some guy with long hair came around a few times. That didn't last long. The last time he was over, he was real upset when he left. That was just before the boy went missing."

David's body stiffened and he felt his stomach churn. "Did you know his name?"

"Never met him, but he had a sign on the door of his truck with a phone number. Let me think." He pinched his lips between his thumb and forefinger, then added, "Can't remember the phone number, but I think it said, 'Jake's Garage.'"

CHAPTER 28

Todd O'Malley rubbed his chin as he sat in the secondhand recliner in his studio apartment. Having finished his Wendy's hamburger and fries, he balled up the paper bag and tossed it at an overflowing wastepaper basket. He missed and didn't bother to pick it up. He needed to figure out what to do about Guy Falcone's mother. She was trouble.

Sure, he was glad that Guy never gave him up to the police as his supplier, but that did not mean he owed him anything. Not one fucking thing. He banged his fist on the arm of his chair. In fact, he was still pissed. He remembered talking to Guy on the phone through the glass when he visited prison. "What's the down side?" he had argued. "You'd sell lots of bags in here."

"No, no selling smack. Not ever again. I've got a son, and he needs a father." Todd had called him a fucking idiot! And talk about pissed! His mother wouldn't deal either. Then she didn't want him selling at the nursing home. Like she could order him around. The Falcone family better watch their step; they were on thin ice with him.

He decided he'd try reasoning with that Falcone bitch one more time. Figure out what would make her back off. Maybe even get generous, offer her a bone. And if that didn't work, he knew how to work her over.

Todd saw himself as a man of action and felt better after he had decided on a plan. He whipped his jacket from the back of the chair and thrust his arms into it. He retrieved his cap from the closet—the one with the Patriots' logo—and put it on backwards. Next, he took a shoe box from the shelf, removed a handgun and stuffed it in his pocket. Finally he shoved his feet into his leather boots. He was ready.

In his Dodge Dart, he drove to Sunny Days nursing home, where Guy's mother would be working the supper shift. The front door was locked, which made sense after dark. He rang the bell. Wondering where Gwendolyn Grey had gotten herself to that day, he was uncomfortable still carrying her packets of smack in his pocket. If he had a kid, he wouldn't send him to *that* day care, for sure. He shifted his weight from one foot to the other waiting for someone to answer the bell. The chime was loud; some goddamn idiot must have heard it. Finally, it was answered by a twenty-year-old woman with cropped hair, wearing scrubs with a flowered top and green pants.

"Todd, what are you doing here?"

He couldn't remember her name. T something, Tammy or Theresa or Tiffany. He gave her his best smile. "How you doing?" When she didn't respond, he said, "I want to talk to Mrs. Falcone."

"She's busy making dinner for the residents." Not only didn't she move to allow him in, but she also thrust out her hip and screwed up her face, as if to say, "Waiting for you to leave."

The little twerp, wanting to exert her power; he knew he'd have to play it humble. He removed his cap. "I'll be real quick. Won't interrupt what she's doing." Fingering the cap, he turned it in a circle.

"Come back later, after they've eaten."

"Would if I could, but…" he quickly thought of a lie, "I've got to pick up my daughter. She's only two." He indicated her height with his hand.

She looked thoughtful, then stepped aside. "Be sure you don't take long." "Down that hall and to the left."

An antiseptic smell irritated his nose and caused him to cough as he hurried down the hallway. In the kitchen, the odor was less intense and mixed with oregano, hamburger and tomatoes. Steam was rising from a pot, and Mrs. Falcone's back was to him when he entered.

He realized she must have heard him, because she turned around while rolling a meatball over and over in her hands. She paused and scowled at him. "What do you want?"

"To talk to you."

"Can't you see I'm working?"

"It'll only take a minute."

"Haven't got one to spare." Having finished rounding out the meatball, she placed it on a plate. Then she moved the platter of hamburger to a side counter. At first her action puzzled him, but then he grinned, figuring she was afraid of him. Didn't want her back to him.

Replacing his hat, he said, "Look, this is one of the places I hustle for money. I'm a dealer and I can't quit coming here. It's business."

She snorted, wiped sweat from her forehead with her apron, picked up a portion of meat and began rolling it while facing him. "Only three people here buy your junk. I know for a fact, that's true. You can drop that many."

Her reaction pissed him off. Stupid cow. This was not going to be easy. "I'm coming here, so you mother-fucking bitch, you better get used to it." She took a step back.

The doorbell chimed. There was a soft echo of the sound in the hallway.

"Guy'll never see a jail cell again. I'll see to that. My grandson's gonna know his father. I'll see to that too. Spend lots of time with him. And you're not gonna threaten that. Stay away from him and me." She stepped back. Taking a pack of cigarettes from her apron pocket, she tapped one out and lit it. She inhaled while staring at him, then slowly blew smoke through her nose. "Don't come 'round here no more. Get used to that. Maybe Guy didn't want to snitch on you, but I don't mind."

Todd felt the hair prick up on the back of his neck. Maybe she was bluffing. But if she wasn't afraid, she would be in a second. He hunched up his shoulders, pulled out the gun, stepped toward her and grabbed the front of her blouse. Her eyes widened and she dropped the cigarette on the floor.

Voices and footsteps were in the hallway. Two cops appeared in the kitchen, one tall with thin eyes. Both drew their guns. "Drop your weapon and step away from her."

Todd let the gun fall to the floor as Madeline Falcone hustled to the side of one of the cops, her face drained of all color. She pointed a finger at Todd. "This low life was trying to get me to sell drugs. Here! Can you believe it? Maybe you should check him out to see what he's got on him."

Anger and fear flashed through Todd. Gwendolyn's stash in his pockets and the revolver on the floor. The Asian cop patted him down and took the two packets from his pocket. "You're under arrest," he said, taking his handcuffs from his duty belt.

CHAPTER 29

Twilight had become night and the air felt heavy. Jake started his truck and waved at the last of the volunteers at Ropewalk Court who were pulling away in a car. Before backing up, Jake wondered where Will was. He remembered how… well, exhausted, Jackie had looked when Becky helped her from the field. Becky was a customer of his, a good person. Jackie used to bring Will to the garage when she needed service. Nice little kid. After dating her a few times, she had decided not to see him again, and he had cursed at her. He had apologized afterward, but he doubted she was a customer anymore.

He pulled a toothpick from the glove compartment, stuck it in his mouth and drove into the street. Since his clothes were dirty from the search, he swung by the drive-through at MacDonald's for a Coke and Quarter Pounder, but only managed a few bites. Constantly anxious about his declining business, he knew he wouldn't be able to sleep, so he decided to return to the garage and work on his classic Ford.

When he parked behind the building, he was surprised to find the bay door wide open. Light from the garage tumbled onto the ground outside. Hadn't he locked it when he left this afternoon to run some errands? He couldn't remember, but he was usually careful about that. He reached for his cell phone to call the police, but he could not get reception. Maybe he should drive to the police station. But goddammit! Someone had broken into his property. His! And no one was going to get away with that! He clicked open the glove compartment and removed a pistol before stepping from the truck.

Even though he moved cautiously, gravel crunched beneath his boots, announcing his approach. He hid in shadow near the corner of the entrance and listened. An overhead bulb on the ceiling inside made a bizz-bizz-bizz sound like a mosquito. A car droned past on the road out front. Bizz-bizz-bizz. He waited. The call of a mourning dove.

Finally, he gathered courage, and fearful that it might be his last act, he poked his head in. Everything was as he had left it: papers strewn on the desk, the creeper off to one side, tools sprawled on the cement floor near his Ford.

He ducked inside, pointed the gun in front of him as he had seen in the movies and crept around the car. He sniffed a faint copper odor before he saw the blood. He expected there would be more. In the center of the mess, a woman lay on her side. Her face was stark white. The side of her skull was bashed in—a hammer beside her head—one of his. She was tall. Her clothes were spattered in blood: white silk jacket, tan linen slacks, heels. A braid curved down her back, tied with a bright crimson ribbon, fouled where it dipped into the blood.

Numbness flooded his body as his mind struggled to take in the horror. Then he saw them. Bloody paw prints tracked across the floor to the steel shelving against the far wall. When he investigated, he found traces of blood on a carburetor and on a brake disc. He searched his entire shop, but there was no one to be found, and no cat.

Perspiring in spite of the cool evening, he rubbed the palm of his hand over his face. Who on earth would want to kill a woman in his garage? He didn't know the answer to that. He rolled the creeper over to the body and was glad he could not see her face. Even though he was shaking badly, he managed to haul her on, but then realized how unwise it would be to roll the body outside. He decided instead to back his truck into the garage. After lowering the tailgate, he hefted her into the bed. Damn, she was heavy. Then he covered her with a tarp.

While he secured the bay door, he wondered what he should do next. Soon, the evening rush hour traffic would clear. He would wait. But then what? He flipped off the light and sat in the dark, pondering what he should do.

CHAPTER 30

Joey LeBrun wondered if he had heard it, but then dismissed the sound as a stray animal or even the wind. On the radio, the Stylistics were belting out "You Make Me Feel Brand New." A parent had called and said she was stuck in a conference at work. Could she pick up her child later? As usual, Joey had stayed with the child. Now that they were gone, he wondered if he should call Dara Lee instead of Blake for a ride home. Soon, he would buy his own car. He had saved up enough for a down payment. But, it was late and he was hungry. Perhaps he could offer to take her to dinner. He switched off the radio. There it was again.

With the outside light switched on, he peered out the front door window, but saw nothing. He turned on the spotlights that lit up the land adjacent to the day care center, and stepped outside. Wailing. It wasn't the wind. Without a coat, the air was biting, and he shivered. What the hell? In the playground, a toddler was crying hysterically. She was wearing brightly colored pink boots.

CHAPTER 31

After everyone left and the dinner things were cleared away, Kurt and Monica went to their office where they spent a great deal of their time. Each sat in a comfortable leather chair at separate desks. A police scanner was spitting out static.

For the tenth time that day, Kurt Googled a variation on the theme of abduction. This time he entered "vanished" and scanned the results that popped up. In frustration, he tossed his hands in the air. "There's a lot being done, but…"

"It's not enough." Monica finished his thought. "He's still missing." She rested an elbow on her desk with her chin on her fist. She checked the time on her computer screen. "Will must be terrified. Eight o'clock already."

The police scanner crackled. Kurt swiveled in his chair to face her, "I don't see where we can go from here, do you?"

Monica looked at him and sighed. "I really don't. We'll have to wait and see what Zoey learns from Becky's grandmother." She shook her head. "How could someone possibly sell her own child? And who knows what that Kappel woman did with her daughter? I don't even want to think of those possibilities."

They were both silent for a time. "Listen, Monica…" Kurt hesitated. "Sooner or later, we need to talk about having a child."

She leaned back and placed her hands on her abdomen. "Kurt, There's nothing to talk about."

"Would you just look at the adoption papers?"

"There's no point."

"Damn it, Monica. I worry about you. Look at how long it's taking you to recover from that miscarriage."

"I'm feeling fine. You know, I'm not the first woman in the world with diabetes to want her own child. And I won't be the last."

"Monica, if anything happened to you—"

"Nothing will."

"If the baby had birth defects, you'd never forgive yourself."

She stood up. "Want tea?"

His throat tightened. He squeezed his eyes shut, then blinked several times. "I'll get it." He went to the kitchen and flipped the gas on under the kettle. Usually he was patient with her, but the tension of the day had rubbed him raw. Beneath her bluster, he was aware how vulnerable she was, and he wanted, fiercely, to protect her.

The tea kettle blasted a whistle. He switched off the knob and listened to the dying wail as he poured water into cups. Frankly, he felt stumped, both in his effort to bring Monica to her senses and in his attempt to help locate Will. Tonight, the temperature would plummet. He hoped Will was indoors. There must be something else they could do, if only he could think of it.

The police scanner sputtered from the office, and he heard a garbled announcement. When it finished, Monica rushed out with her laptop slung over her shoulder. "That's a homicide. Gotta go." She left Kurt standing with two cups of tea.

CHAPTER 32

That night, Detective Tom Madsen was annoyed because he was enjoying his KFC chicken dinner when he received a call from dispatch. A corpse had been found in the lower parking lot at Plimoth Plantation, where the pathway to the movie entrance was located. Two police officers had secured the scene by cordoning off a perimeter around the body. He was needed. He tossed his half-eaten chicken back in the box, and placed it on the passenger seat. When he arrived at the scene, a spotlight attached to the police vehicle lit up the protected area.

After sliding his crime kit from the passenger side, Madsen greeted the officers who were leaning against the squad car. He slipped paper covers over his shoes and pulled on latex gloves, feeling them snap against his wrists. Then he ducked under the yellow tape. The victim was lying on her back with the left side of her skull battered, but the right was relatively unscathed. Judging from the wound, she had been hit with a fairly heavy object. He hunched over and bagged her hands to preserve any material under her fingernails, in case she had scratched her killer. Rigor mortis had begun to set in, but only in the face and neck, so he figured she hadn't been dead too long. The Medical Examiner would be along soon and make a closer determination.

There was no identification in her pockets and no purse. Blood spattered a silk jacket, white blouse, tan linen slacks and stiletto heels. From the small amount of blood on the pavement, it was obvious she had been moved. When he examined her clothing with a magnifying glass, he found an oily smudge that soiled one of her sleeves. A hair clung to the spot. He retrieved the fiber with a tweezers, inspected it carefully, noting a peach color. After placing it in a bag, he made a notation on the plastic and in a notebook.

Soon, an engine droning grew louder, and a vehicle stopped at the end of the driveway. He looked up. But because of the glaring headlights, he could not tell the make of car, and the driver was only a shadow. One of the cops was striding down to intercept the automobile. Madsen concentrated his focus on the body. After taking a few shots with his camera, he decided to return the next morning when the sun was up. He heard arguing down by the car and recognized Monica's voice. He had encountered her at crime scenes before, and she was one of the few journalists he liked. Also, once, she had been introduced as Zoey's sister at a party.

"Let her through," he called out, and packed up the kit. Monica's boots clicked as she approached him.

"Omigod," she said. When he turned around, she was standing with her hand over her mouth. "I recognize her."

"You know her?" Madsen asked, hoping for information.

"Not exactly. I noticed her at a few business luncheons. Networking kind of things. She looked a bit stiff, no pun intended, but she worked the room pretty good anyway."

He ducked back under the crime scene tape. "Can you tell me her name?"

Monica looked thoughtful. "Not sure if I ever knew her name. Don't remember actually talking to her."

"Too bad. She didn't have any ID on her."

CHAPTER 33

On the second day that Will was missing, Zoey felt worn out and limp as an old bed sheet. She made the long drive from Plymouth to Pepperell that morning. Gloomy and overcast, the weather brought no relief, and her head was pounding. As she drove through the covered bridge on Groton Street in Pepperell, she guessed the Town Hall would be opening right about then. And she did not give a damn if she missed the principal's meeting that day. If she did not go, Zoey suspected he would ask the Board to fire her for insubordination. What an ass!

Perhaps she could have avoided the drive and obtained the information she needed over the phone; however, she wanted to see for herself the dream house Krista Kappel had abandoned so long ago. Touch it, sense it, internalize its whispered messages. She hoped her inner voice, that intuition she relied on, would kick into overdrive and provide a direction, a breakthrough to help find Will.

She had passed farms and mansions with stables, the countryside giving off a feeling of comfort and wealth. The town echoed that ease, although many houses were smaller. She turned off Hollis Street onto Main and parked near the Town Hall.

Zoey found the department for public records where a woman was relaxing behind a desk reading a newspaper. Her gray hair was cut just below her ears and her gold bracelets made a soft jingling sound whenever she turned a page. A maroon blouse was tucked into a black skirt that fell just below her knees. She looked up when Zoey entered the room.

"I'm looking for a property near Sucker Brook. Owned by a man named Kappel."

"Oh, you must mean Walter Kappel." The woman folded the paper carefully, stood, straightened her skirt, and approached the counter. "If you're looking to buy it, you're out of luck."

"Has someone else purchased it?"

"Oh no. It's not that. That property's been vacant a long time, but it's never come on the market."

"I wonder, could you tell me about Walter Kappel?"

"Everyone my age, who's lived here for a while, knew him." She sniffed. "But as a public employee, I can't talk about a private citizen to anyone who walks in here, even if he is dead and buried. I can give you the address. That's a matter of public record."

"Actually, I'm looking for a missing child. Anything you can tell me about the Kappel family might help find him."

The woman fingered her bracelets. "Who did you say you were?"

"Zoey Stone." She extended her hand and smiled. "I teach at a school for troubled kids."

"Oh, a teacher." The woman shook her hand. "I retired after twenty-five years at a public high school. Name's Franny."

"Well, Franny, even if it's just a bit of information, it might help. Something you feel is ethical to tell me."

The woman continued to play with her bracelets. She remained silent.

"Could you tell me what Walter Kappel was like?"

"Likeable. Active in town affairs. Spent money like it was water. He'd walk into a bar and buy everyone drinks."

"You know his wife?"

The woman snorted. "Oh, stuck-up. Never met anyone who thought she was so entitled. But, then, she was movie-star gorgeous. Gives you certain advantages in life. Guess that's why he married her. It certainly wasn't for her personality. After he died, she moved out of town with her two kids. Couldn't get away fast enough." She tucked her hair behind her ear. "Crazy how she hung onto that property. I could understand if she rented it out, but she just left it there. Somebody goes out there, now and then, even after all these years, and takes care of the place. Mows the lawn, that sort of thing."

"Know who it is?"

"No. Never paid that much attention."

"I'd like to see the house."

"It's still private property, but suit yourself." She looked at the bindings of leather bound books scattered over the counter. She opened one and found Walter Kappel's plot.

"That's a lot of land."

"Sure is. It's located off Blue Heron. Borders on conservation land. Lots of privacy." The woman rummaged in her desk, then unfolded a road map on the counter. "Road's not shown on this map." Circling an area with her finger, she said, "Somewhere around here."

"How will I find it?"

"You can take this map. I have others. He had to build a long private road. Named it himself."

"And what address am I looking for?"

"He did put up a mail box if it's still standing. You could look for that." The woman raised one eyebrow. "Called it Devil's Reach Road. Number six."

Zoey thanked the woman in the Pepperell Town Hall as she folded up the map. "Is there a local place people go for breakfast?"

"Sure, try Charlotte's Cozy Kitchen, just up the street."

Stepping out of the building, Zoey was conflicted. She itched for more information about the Kappel family, but she wondered if it would help find Will. She sensed it might be useful. Yet this was the second day he was missing. Perhaps she should check out the mansion quickly and go back to Plymouth. Any waste of time could be critical. After agonizing over the pros and cons, she decided to see if she could discover more about the Kappels.

With the map tucked into her pocketbook, she walked down Main Street and found the restaurant. Small round tables, booths, wooden chairs. Seated alone on a stool at a counter, a woman was eating sausage and eggs. Her face was sun-wrinkled and a silver circle pierced one eyebrow. Settling onto the stool next to her, Zoey studied a menu. "Say, what's good here?"

"Everything. Can't go wrong."

She ordered a muffin and coffee. "Lived here long?"

"All my life."

"I wonder if you could help me. I'm looking for information about the Kappel family."

"That's going back some."

"Did you know Walter?"

"Pretty good. What's your interest in him?"

"A child has gone missing. There could be a connection to that family. Any information might help."

"Really? That doesn't seem possible after all these years." The woman scratched her head. "Well, he's dead, so I guess it doesn't matter much what's said. We shared an interest in horses. Walter liked Arabians. Used to board one at my stable. His wife didn't want it on their property. She wanted nothing to do with any animal."

"What was he like?"

"Nice enough. A bit eccentric, but I liked him. He was more social than his wife."

"Eccentric how?" Zoey buttered her muffin.

"Dressed a bit loud. Had the feeling he was a needy sort of person. Wanted everyone's attention. Told lots of jokes. But, he's been dead a long time. I don't see how this could help."

"What was their relationship like?"

"That I couldn't tell you. I only talked horses with him. I'd see her in town once in a while. I don't think she had any friends. Kind of a sad existence, don't you think?"

"What about the property near Sucker Brook."

"If you're interested in buying that, you'd have to track down his twins."

"Twins?"

"Yeah. A boy and a girl. I heard his widow died recently. Of course, everything would go to them." The woman finished her sausages and dusted off her hands.

"What happened to that Arabian after he died?"

"Wife sold it." She fingered the ring in her eyebrow. "Walter was awfully nervous when I last saw him. Wasn't like him. Right after he died, rumors were flying around town about him owing the wrong people money. About the car wreck not being an accident."

Zoey felt a chill run through her.

CHAPTER 34

Becky had intended to go home, but she spent the night dozing in the armchair in Jackie's living room. The next morning, when she awoke, Jackie was still asleep on the futon. After deciding to stay until Jackie was awake, she wrapped herself in a blanket, went outside and sat in one of the plastic chairs on the porch with a cup of peppermint tea. She didn't know what Jackie's state of mind would be when she realized Will was still missing. As a nurse, Becky had seen people react to tragedy and most did not manage it well. Soon, she was aware of movement in the house, the door creaked open and Jackie stepped onto the porch. Her eyes looked haunted with dark circles underneath. She still wore the clothes she had slept in.

"Want breakfast?"

Jackie shook her head and sank into the other plastic chair on the porch. "I just called the police. There's nothing new."

Becky heard the grinding of the minivan before it boiled into the driveway and lurched to a stop. When Guy exploded from the driver's seat, every muscle in Becky's body tensed.

He bounded to the bottom of the steps. "Guy…" Jackie said hesitantly. Becky watched him soften like ice cream left out too long.

Trembling, Jackie stood up. At the same time, Guy leaped up the steps, gently pulled Jackie to him and enfolded her in his arms. She leaned into him. Becky took a step toward them, but stopped herself. Instinct told her to protect Jackie from Guy, but she also knew the choice was Jackie's and not hers. Together, the couple sobbed, united in their loss, as Becky looked away.

After some time, Jackie caught her breath. "We have to look for him."

Becky moved closer to Jackie and placed her hand on her arm, ignoring Guy. "Maybe you should wait here. Will might be found soon. You know he'll need you."

"I must do something. I can't just do nothing." She punched her fist into her thigh.

The three of them were silent for a time. Jackie and Guy clung to each other, while Becky stood apart, shuffling from one foot to the other. "Of course, you have to do something. Go. I'll stay." Becky retrieved the blanket and sat back down. The chair's plastic arm was split, and she picked at the broken piece. Without looking up, she asked, "Got your cell phone?"

"No, I don't." Jackie hurried across the porch and back into the house. The door slammed. Becky looked up as Guy retreated down the steps. For a moment, he stopped, turned, and gazed back at her. "Thanks," he said abruptly. Then he climbed in and started the truck. Jackie hurried past her and pulled herself up into the cab. When they drove off, Becky noticed a vehicle that had been parked across the street; it started up and followed them. She could not see who was driving.

CHAPTER 35

As Guy drove the van away from the apartment, Jackie's eyes were already sweeping the surroundings for her son.

"If Will ran away, where would he go?"

Jackie bristled in the passenger seat beside him. "He wouldn't do that."

Shit. He hadn't wanted to offend her. In spite of the anger that gnawed at him because she had stopped visiting him in prison, he thought of her constantly, and pictured them living together. "All little boys run away at some point. It's an adventure. I know, I did."

"Well, I'm not like your mother. He wanted to be with me all the time."

"Goddamn it, Jackie—I said *if*. Work with me, will you?" He immediately regretted being so gruff.

"What if you were an abductor, where would you hide him?"

Guy didn't say anything for a full minute. "I didn't take him, Jackie." He wasn't so sure about his mother, but he wasn't going to tell her that. He'd handle that in his own way. "Would he hide in a graveyard? Maybe think it was funny?"

"Turn up this street." She pointed left. "He wouldn't do that. He'd be too afraid of the dead bodies buried there."

Driving in silence, they scanned houses, driveways and front yards—desperate for a clue as to his whereabouts.

"I never thought you did. Take him, I mean." She added, "He might pretend he's a Wampanoag and run on the foot path that passes by the Grist Mill. We used to go there. To get ice cream at the Mill. He'd always get strawberry with sprinkles, in one of those big waffle cones, you know the ones." She started to cry.

"We'll find him." Guy reached out and placed his hand over hers. He was glad she didn't pull away. He wanted to believe what Dara Lee had told him—that Jackie still loved him. Go slow, he told himself. He knew that's what he needed to do, for his sake as well as hers. Prison had wounded him deeply, and he was terrified of what he might do if she abandoned him again. He withdrew his hand. "We're almost at the Mill. Should we look around?"

"It would be a waste of time. I know my own son. He didn't run away."

He wanted to correct her and say "our son," but he didn't.

"Take a right here." Jackie shifted in her seat. "If I remember correctly, there were a couple of sheds up by the lake, if they're still there. Good place to hide a child."

"I used to swim there. Sure don't remember any sheds."

"Not by the beach, farther up. Kinda out of the way. In the woods."

Guy nosed his truck up Billington Street and, after a few blocks, pulled onto a dirt road that jostled them both. When the road narrowed and became impassable, he parked.

They trudged up the path toward the lake and soon saw patches of sand visible through tall grasses near the water. Broken rungs on a life guard tower hung at odd angles, rendering it useless. A hole yawned open in the side of an abandoned kayak. "Sure don't remember it like this."

The trail followed the lake and then veered off into the woods, which became denser as they moved away from the water. As they continued, the path disappeared altogether and, unsure what to do, they halted in the midst of the overgrown vegetation.

Jackie stood with her back toward the path. "We were going this way, so maybe if we continued in this direction…" She held her arm straight out in front of her.

"Even if a shed's out here, there'd be no way to get to it. Nobody would be using it. We should go back."

"If it's so remote, all the more reason to use it."

Branches snapped behind them and he saw Jackie freeze. Adrenaline rushed through Guy's body. Hunching down, he waited. Nothing. All he could hear was their breathing. Slowly, he crept in the direction of the sound, cringing at the noise he was making. He found newly trampled growth, but he was afraid to leave Jackie too far behind. He backtracked and said, "A harmless animal," but he sensed she did not believe him.

CHAPTER 36

Zoey drove by twice before she spotted the gap in the trees on Blue Heron Road. When she climbed from her car, she found a wooden post rotting on the ground with a mailbox still attached. She stooped down and brushed dirt from the black metal. Specks of paint remained, but she could not make out a number or any letters. However, according to her map, this was number six Devil's Reach Road, right on the edge of conservation land. Grass-filled ruts were all that was left of the road. The crushed grass was still green, leading her to the conclusion that someone must have driven down recently, but who? Krista had hired a caretaker for the property, but according to that woman in The Depot, she had been dead for over a year. So who was using the road?

Driving on the ruts jarred her back and bruised her tailbone; trees and bushes on both sides of the Wrangler scratched its paint. Zoey hoped she wouldn't meet anyone. If she did, she had planned to explain her trespass by saying she was looking to buy property in Pepperell. At the end of the so-called road, the woods gave way to a well-kept lawn which showcased the mansion. What a surprise! If she were standing in Georgia in the 1800s, she would call the mansion a plantation house. So this was the dream house. She had expected something more modern, but maybe Krista had pictured herself as a southern belle. Zoey parked near the front where white columns announced the importance of the home.

Steps led to a wraparound veranda. At a tall window, she rubbed a circle of dirt from a pane and peered into what must have been a living room. It appeared to be in decent condition with all the furniture in place. In contrast to the style of the house, the décor was modern. She imagined Krista relaxing on the couch, snuggled up with a book, the children playing on the rug. What had it felt like when she'd realized her life was a lie? To suddenly lose her husband, discover he was bankrupt? Certainly, she must have wondered if he had been a criminal himself.

Walking the circumference of the house, she understood the appeal to someone like Krista. The woods protected her privacy and the place was completely isolated. When she rounded the corner to the back of the house, Zoey stopped and caught her breath at the beauty of Sucker Brook. Trees along the bank displayed their autumn colors and were reflected in the clear water. An empty wine glass sat on a side table between wooden chairs with colorful cushions. She wished Will weren't missing. She wished she could slip into one of those chairs, kick off her shoes and spend the day watching water ripple past, but of course, she couldn't.

As she circled back to the front, she noticed how well-kept the outside of the mansion was. In a few places, paint was peeling from wooden pillars, but the vinyl siding looked new. There was evidence of recent repairs: some planks on the porch floor had been replaced, and new stain had been applied.

Hoping to gain access, she tried the windows but found them secured. However, on one, the screws on both the sash lock and keeper were loose. Also, fortunately, the lock had barely hooked the metal lip on the keeper. She banged the frame and jiggled it. It took a while, but the lock jerked a bit to the left. As she continued to bump the window up and down, back and forth, the lock finally gave way and the window opened. She climbed through and discovered she was in a den. The room smelled musty as if it had been closed up forever. Fearful that someone might be inside, she tiptoed across the hardwood floor and eased open the door. Thank goodness it moved noiselessly on its hinges. She found herself in the living room where a baby grand piano dominated one corner of the room. The lid was closed and covered with dust, and many photos rested on its surface. The frames were expensive with intricate carvings. They, too, were dusty as well as the glass covering the pictures. Zoey examined each one of them and was surprised to find a few with names scrawled across the subjects. After deciding to remove one photo, she folded it and tucked it into her pocket. She crossed the room. As she placed her hand on a banister with her body poised to go upstairs, she heard a motor chug outside. Flinching, she listened for the direction of the sound and determined it was coming from the brook. Hustling back through the den, she left the door ajar in her haste and scrambled through the window. She raced for her Jeep. The engine noise grew louder, and her fear of being caught intensified. As she started the Wrangler, she wondered if there was a dock she had missed spotting at the rear of the house. Driving as fast as she dared on those ruts, she bounced down Devil's Reach Road.

On her way back to Plymouth, she thought about Krista's tragedy and how it must have twisted her mind. By holding onto that property, she had never had to admit the depth of her losses, never fully feel the pain. In maintaining the house, she kept a memory alive: the ghost of the woman she had been. But no matter how hard she tried, Zoey could not wrap her mind around the selling of her son.

All the way home, she agonized, hoping she hadn't been off on a wild goose chase. If her sister was wrong, if the crime of selling children was not related to Will's abduction, precious time had been squandered. How awful she would feel if Will had been harmed while she was driving around Pepperell for no reason. Pieces of what she had learned and seen tumbled over and over in her mind. When she arrived at her apartment, she knew what she had to do.

CHAPTER 37

Even though Jackie feared what might be lurking in the bushes, she insisted Guy slog ahead with her in an attempt to find the sheds where Will could be hidden. Reluctantly, he followed. Both were alert, checking behind them and to the sides.

It happened suddenly. Guy cried out and she heard a sickening thud. A pain shot up her arm as it was twisted behind her back. She fell to her knees next to Guy who lay limp on the ground. Trembling, she reached to check on him, but was jerked back. "What're you doing out here with a convicted felon?"

She heard a rage she had never encountered before, like a growl from an enraged animal. It frightened her, and she tried to clear her head of the fear and figure out what to do, how to deal with Blake.

He shook her and she cried out. "I said what the hell are you doing?"

"Will," was all she could think of to say. Pebbles were digging into her knees.

"What do you mean, Will?" She saw a deep gash on Guy's head. Losing focus, his eyes closed and he lost consciousness. Blake released his grip on her arm, and she tried again to check on Guy. "Leave him." His tone terrified her and she froze.

When Guy regained consciousness, his wound was throbbing, and a dull ache filled his head. It was sprinkling rain, but his clothes were drenched, and he wondered how long he had been out. When he stood up, he felt dizzy and pain shot up his leg, but he managed to stay upright. Muddled, he tried to focus, figure out exactly where he was, and which direction would bring him out of the woods. And where the fuck was Jackie? He yelled her name, which caused a stabbing sensation behind his eyes. She didn't answer. Terrified, he knew he had to find her.

CHAPTER 38

Shaken by the sight of the corpse at Plimoth Plantation, Monica had not slept well, nor had Kurt. In the night, he had thrashed about and pulled the blanket from her several times. Outside, the temperature had nose-dived; she worried about Will and prayed that he was somewhere warm.

Finally, she dropped off to sleep and woke in the early afternoon. Kurt was gone. Annoyed that her husband had let her sleep so late, she shuffled to the kitchen to find him and tell him exactly that, only to discover a note saying he would get in touch with her later. "Humph!" she said out loud, and decided not to call his cell phone.

After dressing in leather slacks with matching jacket, she stood in front of the open refrigerator and ate cold leftovers from the night before. Normally, she would be more selective in what she ate, but she felt the press of time because Will was still missing. Wanting to find out what Becky's grandmother had told her sister, she drove to Zoey's apartment, hoping she wouldn't be in one of her pissy moods. When Zoey answered the door, looking exhausted, her mouth tightened into a thin line when she saw Monica on the porch." Woke on the wrong side of the bed?" Monica asked.

Zoey didn't respond. As they climbed the stairs to the apartment, Monica smelled the aroma of chicken and dill. Jealousy struck her, because the one thing Zoey surpassed her at was cooking; at least, that was the one thing Monica would admit to. Although she couldn't consciously articulate, even to herself, Zoey's superiority in other areas, she had vague suspicions they existed.

When they entered the kitchen, she was surprised to see David Roth pouring soup into bowls. "Are you two back together?"

"Grab a bowl if you want my famous chicken-a-la-noodle." He smiled and bowed with a flourish, ladle in hand.

Monica laughed, and then noticed the chopped carrots and bits of celery on the counter, along with freshly made noodles. Homemade! "Thanks, but I just ate." She was glad the soup wasn't Zoey's. "I had a terrible experience with a dead body yesterday."

"Your sister was just telling me what she found out."

Between spoonfuls of warm soup, Zoey explained what she had learned from Maggie Armstrong the night before and her trip that morning. "Krista Kappel lived in her dream house in Pepperell with her husband and twins, a boy and girl. When her husband died in a suspicious car crash, rumors spread about his possible criminal behavior. Not being well liked in town, she moved to Quincy with her children. That's where she met Becky's grandmother, Maggie Armstrong.

"However, Krista never sold the home in Pepperell. In fact, she kept it as if everything had frozen the day her husband died." Zoey massaged her temple. "Had a weird address—number six Devil's Reach Road."

David shifted in his seat. "Wonder who gave it that address, the husband or Krista?"

"There's that 'six' again. What is the obsession with that number?" Monica drummed her fingers on the table.

Zoey took three photographs from her pocketbook and handed them to her sister. "Becky's grandmother had two of these pictures of the family, taken when the twins were toddlers. One is the twins alone; the other shows them with their mother. That one is a bit out of focus, and there's something wrong in that picture, but I can't put my finger on it. The folded one is Walter Kappel."

"These twins look familiar."

"I thought so too. Then came the part you researched, Monica. Krista masqueraded as an adoption agency, abducted five babies and sold them along with her toddler son. Then there's the disappearance of her daughter."

Monica felt her stomach twist as a sour taste rose from her belly and slipped over her tongue. "Selling her own son."

"She was arrested, made bail and vanished."

"Maybe she saw the arrest coming, and asked someone to care for her daughter, then collected her after she skipped out." David poured the remaining soup into a glass bowl and covered it with plastic wrap. "Or, she may have sold her too, and no one discovered that sale."

"I think the mother has reappeared." Monica noticed her sister had a smug look on her face, subtle, but it was there.

"Impossible. She died. The house belongs to the twins."

Feeling challenged, Monica sat up straighter in the chair, adjusted her shoulders, and raised her chin in the air. "So, Miss Know-It-All, identify the person in this room who discovered the twenty-year-old adoption scheme." Monica raised her hand. "Me, that's who."

"Please. I give you credit for that. You are an excellent investigative reporter. However-"

David didn't let her finish the thought. "Hey Monica, what did you start to say about a corpse?"

Scowling at her sister, Monica made a popping sound with her mouth and sat sideways in the chair so her back was mostly toward Zoey. Then she explained about the woman being found with no identification and how tall and movie-star-beautiful she must have been. Before she had finished, her cell phone rang. Kurt's name popped up on the caller ID. "Hi love." As she listened to her husband, she found herself wondering, what on earth was happening.

She hung up. "Can you believe this? Guy was attacked. A motorist found him on the side of a road. He's in the hospital, but he'll be okay. Something about a nasty gash. Now Jackie's missing."

In the same instance, Zoey and David reacted.

"What!? Any idea what happened to her?"

"Does he know who attacked him?"

"The answer to both questions is Blake. Apparently, Guy saw him twisting Jackie's arm before he lost consciousness."

Zoey bolted up from her chair. "That woman who was murdered. You said she was gorgeous and tall. Did she have long black hair, so long that it was probably never cut?"

"Yes, but how did—"

"A photo I saw at the house in Pepperell. Jackie is in terrible danger. David, how fast can you drive?" Zoey headed for the door. "I'll explain on the way." As all three raced down the stairs, Zoey asked, "Do you still have the gun in your glove compartment?"

CHAPTER 39

Blake's eyes shone with a wildness. Sweat dampened his forehead, and he wiped the back of his hand across his face. "You were looking for Will?"

"Y…Yes."

"You didn't need to go with that convict. I could have helped you. Why didn't you ask me?"

"I didn't look for him. He showed up at my apartment."

"So what? You could have told him to get lost."

Her eyes moistened and her hands shook. "I want my Will back."

Blake was quiet for a while as she sobbed. "He's fine. I know where he is. I'll take you to him." He pulled her up.

"But how…" She stopped herself. It was best not to press him about how he knew. "Is he okay?"

"He's fine. He'll be glad to see you." Relief spread through her. He smiled at her, and she forced herself to smile back.

Blake led Jackie from the woods, confident she would soon see him as the hero that he was. After all, he had found Will. He was the one reuniting mother and son, just as he had always planned to do. Too bad there had been a few glitches along the way, but those were taken care of now. He'd been a little rough with her back there in the woods, but that would pass. After all, she shouldn't have been with an ex-con, and when she acknowledged how wrong she was, he could forgive her. Jackie was his and the three of them would be together. Everyone would realize that was how it was supposed to be.

As he drove to the Hearth & Home motel, he was proud she was his woman, by his side, right there in the passenger seat—quiet, but that was all right with him. Soon enough, she'd be her old chatty self. Before he parked in the lot, he told her, with a smile, to stay in the truck; and she hadn't argued, which was a good sign.

Blake climbed the stairs with a spring in his step. He cricked his neck, left, then right, and found room 203. Whistling, he inserted the key card in the slot. The door opened easily.

Will was sitting on the bed, cross-legged. Next to him was a crumpled McDonald's bag along with two empty cartons of milk. On TV, Scooby Doo was shivering with fear in Shaggy's arms inside a scary mansion. Will rolled over to the edge and his feet plopped to the floor. "Are we going to surprise Mommy now? I'm tired of this game. I want to go home."

"Yeah. It's time to surprise Mommy."

Will took his jacket from the chair. "Did you know there are cats next door? When I meow, they answer me."

Blake grabbed his arm before he could bolt out the door. Will looked up at him. "I didn't like that lady. She wasn't very nice. She left me alone. I don't think she knew how to take care of me."

As soon as Jackie saw them leave the room, she raced across the lot and up the stairs. Will catapulted into her arms. "Are you surprised, Mommy? Did you think the game was fun? Why are you crying?" Blake cracked his knuckles. Jackie hadn't stayed in the truck as he had instructed her.

Later, it began to drizzle and the wind picked up. As Blake drove off Route 3 onto 113, adrenaline pumped through him. Jackie would love where he was bringing her, there was no need to go anywhere else. Everything she could possibly want was right there in the mansion. She could home-school Will, who was a pain in the ass sometimes, but not a bad kid. Blake could put up with him. Sure that this house would fix everything, he glanced at Jackie, who was cradling Will in her lap. Should be buckled in the back seat but, for now, he'd go easy on her. If he saw a cop, he'd order Will to duck down. Looking exhausted, she was listening to her son babble on about the last two days. Certainly not her usual energetic self, but look what she had been through. When she was rested and realized what a gift he had given her, their world would be different.

CHAPTER 40

Rain had been sprinkling for a while as they bounded into David's car, Monica in back and Zoey up front. He pulled away from the curb and asked, "Where are we going?"

"To Pepperell."

David set his GPS.

Zoey's pulse was pounding. "To the dream house," She continued. She turned part way around so she could see her sister. "The body you saw last night was Gwendolyn Grey, owner of the Teddy Bear Day Care. Blake LeBrun was her twin."

"Twin! That can't be! How can you possibly think that?"

"One of the windows was loose on that mansion in Pepperell, so I managed to climb in. Pictures of Blake and Gwendolyn were all over the living room. Not just as babies, but at all ages, even as adults. Gwendolyn's hair fell way below her waist. In some photos, the resemblance between the mother and daughter was remarkable. Unusually beautiful women.

"In one of the photos, the name Gwendolyn was written across the daughter. Monica, when you talked about the corpse who was gorgeous and had usually long hair, all the pieces clicked into place."

"What about the last name of Grey."

"Maybe the daughter was divorced, or maybe she just changed her name for some reason." Zoey rubbed the back of her neck. "No doubt they lived together, so Krista Kappel must have kept her daughter. After she sold the children, she probably saw trouble coming and arranged for someone to care for the girl until she could reunite with her."

"So Blake was the son who was sold." David turned onto Route 3.

"Yes. Krista must have kept track of her son and secretly photographed him. All photos of him are from a distance. One was taken through a chain link fence. In another, half the shot was a corner of a building. You get the idea. There are no photos of the two of them together. Until recently, I don't believe he knew he had been sold like a piece of merchandise.

"And Krista must have returned to the house occasionally, probably to keep alive the fantasy of what her perfect life had been before her husband was killed. When she died recently, the house went to the twins. Since Gwendolyn owned only half, she had to find her brother in order to take possession. The land alone has got to be worth a fortune." Zoey grabbed the door handle as David accelerated. The road was wet and she held her breath. When he had passed a line of cars, she eased her grip. For a moment she watched the wipers squeak across the windshield, and then twisted her body back toward her sister. "Since Gwendolyn grew up with her mother, she knew the family history, and, more than likely shared it with her twin brother."

For a few moments, Monica gazed out the window. "He must have been stunned when he found out he had been sold. That would devastate anyone."

"It may have pushed him over an edge. Although he hid it well, he was unstable to begin with," Zoey said. "Might have inherited it from his mother. That's why Jackie left him. He was becoming more controlling and demanding. And then he wouldn't accept the breakup, which was beginning to frighten her. He was practically stalking her."

"But why would Blake kill his long lost twin?"

"Maybe he was enraged because the mother got rid of him and kept his sister. Only Blake would know the reason why. But I'm sure it was him."

"That intuition again?" David asked. "But why would he go to Pepperell?"

"It's his house now; it is remote and hard to find. Perhaps it gives him a sense of safety, maybe he feels his roots are there. After all, it is the first place he lived with his biological family."

David hit his hand on the steering wheel. "Hey, why the hell didn't we think of this before? Would one of you get in touch with the Pepperell police and explain the situation?"

Monica called and talked to the cop who answered. When she finished, she asked Zoey for the three photos in her pocketbook and, then examined them closely

"Maybe, for some reason, Blake felt he needed to control his twin, so he killed her." David honked the horn and changed lanes. "Where is Will?"

"That's a kind of ultimate control, taking someone's life, isn't it?" Zoey pushed a strand of hair behind her ear.

"This third photo must be the husband. The twins take after their mother. I don't see anything of him in their features."

Zoey put the photos back in her pocketbook. "Will is probably at the house in Pepperell, or with Blake and Jackie. Since he isn't Blake's son, I'm afraid for his safety."

CHAPTER 41

As David sped toward Pepperell, they all grew quiet, each with their own thoughts. Zoey kept rubbing her temples to ease the pressure and then massaged the muscles in her neck. She knew Jackie was smart and, in spite of her fear, would cooperate with Blake and keep Will calm—that is, if he was with them. The unknown was Blake's state of mind. He had murdered his twin. Even though she was sure that Jackie was pretending to go along with him, he must suspect she was doing it under duress.

It seemed to take forever, but finally David turned onto Devil's Reach Road. It must have poured the night before, because the automobile slogged through mud, frustrating Zoey with its slow pace. At the end of the road, she saw Blake's truck parked halfway to the mansion. When David tried to drive closer, the wheels spun, spitting up bits of mud as they dug in deeper. "We'll have to go the rest of the way on foot," He said, removing his gun from the glove compartment and tucking it into his pocket. "Where the hell are the police?"

The weather had worsened. Zoey felt rain sting her face and the wind keened around the trees, giving her an eerie feeling. Chill penetrated her clothes. Hoping no one would glance out a window, all three raced across the lawn, following Blake's tire tracks. They kept the truck between them and the line of vision from the house, as best as they could. Zoey heard Monica curse, so she slowed and looked back. In her high heeled boots, Monica had lost her footing on the slick grass and fallen, but she was scrambling up now, apparently unhurt. So Zoey kept running.

When she reached the truck, she pressed her back against the cab, took deep breaths, and made sure her legs were hidden by the wheels. They, too, had dug into the grass and were mired in mud. Mentally she measured the distance to the front door. It was a long sprint. Water dripped from her eyebrows, and she could taste the rain. David was already at the house, trying to turn the front door knob. Praying that she could make it without being noticed, Zoey dashed across the remaining distance, feeling exposed and vulnerable. She hurried up the porch steps and leaned against the door frame. David mouthed "locked," just as Monica caught up with them. They waited for any sign that they had been detected, but there was no sound of movement near the door, no disturbance inside.

"Let's try that unlocked window I found this morning," Zoey whispered. "Follow me." Flattening her body against the house, she inched her way across the porch, feeling the edges of the vinyl planks against her back. At the first window, she froze when she heard someone talking inside. Although she could not make out the words, she recognized the voice as Jackie's. Closing her eyes, she bit her lip and felt the thud of her heart. After gathering courage, she crouched down and began crawling beneath the window. The floorboards were hard against her knees and she smelled fresh paint on the wood.

Then she heard another voice—Blake's. Again the words were garbled, but his tone was agitated, and Zoey felt a rush of fear for Jackie and Will. As she passed under the sill, she heard the lock click, and the dull sound of a window opening. Every muscle stiffened and she didn't dare breathe. Silence behind her. David and Monica must have noticed it too. In the dampness, her leg muscles cramped, and she bit the inside of her cheek as a counterirritant to the pain. When footsteps retreated inside, she flexed her muscles as best she could, to relieve her discomfort. She waited. Why wasn't anyone talking? Had they been discovered? The quiet was long and unbearable.

Finally, she cocked her head up and saw there was room beyond that window to stand before going on to the second one. In spite of the spasms, she forced her legs to move. When she sensed she had crept far enough, she checked to see if she had safely cleared the window, and then straightened up. She kneaded her muscles and stretched her legs. Looking back, she saw David and Monica had resumed crawling on their hands and knees. Respect mixed with the ambivalent feelings she felt for her sister. Those leather slacks would never be the same.

Again, she crouched down and crawled beneath the next window, unable to avoid a shallow puddle that had formed where the boards angled slightly toward the house; she felt the moisture saturate her knees. When she was under the third window, once again she heard Jackie's voice, just a faint murmur by then.

She rounded the curve in the wraparound porch and then, to be certain she was beyond the living room, continued another ten feet before pushing herself up. Thank goodness! She was next to the unlocked window that she had climbed through earlier that day. Slowly, she pushed the sash upward until the opening was wide enough to slink through. Peering in, she realized she had not shut the door to the den when she'd left earlier that day. Unfortunately, they could be easily seen from the living room. Blake walked by the open door, and a second later, back again. He was pacing. If he had glanced her way, she would have been seen.

She slid down and sat on the porch, leaving the window open. Somehow, they must get inside. David and Monica looked at her quizzically. Taking a quick peek, she saw that Blake was not in view. Quickly, she slung one leg over the sill, ducked her head inside, and as she shifted her weight leaned her body into the den. A scream exploded from the floor above. Zoey fell into the room followed by David who barreled through the opening. A thud sounded from the adjacent living room.

With gun in hand, David sidestepped Zoey as she raced into the living room. Jackie was pushing herself up from the floor; Blake was across the room, gripping the banister of an upper-floor staircase when he saw them. His eyebrows snapped up and his mouth dropped open before he bounded up the stairs, David close behind in pursuit.

Zoey stopped to check on Jackie, who waved her away saying, "I just tripped. Will—upstairs." Overhead, a man yelled, another cursed, someone thumped the floor. Taking the stairs two at a time, Zoey had almost reached the top when a gun discharged. Shock and fear paralyzed her for a second. But then, in spite of the danger, she lurched onto the top stair. Quickly, she assessed the situation. Huge bedroom. Staircase split the room into two sections. Will at one end, crying with the gun in his hand, pointed at the floor. At the other end, Blake and David were tangled like wrestlers at a match. No blood anywhere. But suddenly, Blake wrenched his body free and toppled David to the ground. Like a bulldozer, Blake hurtled himself toward Will and the gun. Over my dead body, Zoey thought. Remembering her martial arts training, she planted herself between Blake and Will. She lifted her right leg high as she pivoted on her left and drove her foot into the side of Blake's neck.

He had underestimated her. Blake's face twisted in fury as he staggered backward, but he managed to regain his balance. But her kick had pushed him away, making space between them. Giving him no time to respond, her two running steps catapulted her into the air, giving her the momentum to thrust her knee into his chest. Both of them tumbled to the floor. She cried out in pain as she landed on her arm and hip. A flash jumped over them and she realized it was David. He snatched the gun from Will's hand, pointed it at Blake and ordered him to stay put. In spite of her pain, Zoey managed to scoot a safe distance away. Blake appeared dazed. Monica and Jackie were at the top of the stairs. Will ran to his mother, who scooped him into her arms. "Find something to tie up Blake," David said. Zoey headed downstairs, and Monica was already on the phone with the police.

CHAPTER 42

W hen Zoey reappeared at the top of the stairs with a long blue rope, David had his gun pointed at Blake, who was lying on his gut on a bed with his hands folded behind his back. His ankles were crossed. Gliding back and forth in a rocking chair, Jackie was whispering to Will, whose face was buried in her shoulder. A bit of color had crept back into her face. Sitting on a window bench, Monica was on the phone with Kurt. Zoey could see that the hand holding the phone was trembling.

"Found this in the garage." She held up the rope for everyone to see, hoping they would feel a bit safer. She wrapped a loop around Blake's wrist, pulled it, and tied a knot.

Blake winced. "That's too tight."

Zoey inspected the rope. "I can move it on your wrist."

"I'm telling you. It's too fucking tight."

"Hey!" Simultaneously, Monica covered the phone and stood up. "Watch it! There's a child here."

Jackie ignored everyone and kept rocking Will.

"You're all right, Blake." Zoey repeated the loop on the other wrist. Running the rope down his back, she said. "Bend your knees." He ignored her, so she wrapped the rope once around both ankles and tugged hard, pulling his feet up several inches. In doing so, the friction against his skin caused the rope to burn, and Blake yelled out, "All right! All right!" In defeat, he bent his knees, and Zoey pulled the rope taut and secured its position with a knot.

"We should all stay up here until the police arrive," she said. "It's easier and safer than trying to move Blake downstairs." Everyone agreed, and Zoey joined her sister on the window bench. She would be bruised and in pain for a while, and so would David, but otherwise they were uninjured. David pulled a chair up close to the bed and kept his gun trained on Blake.

Will straightened up on his mother's lap. "Why did you scream?" she asked.

"Something furry growled at me." He pointed to an opening where a wall intersected the floor. "It went out that hole."

"A mouse?"

Will held his arms out wide. "It was this big."

"Maybe a raccoon."

"Bigger than a raccoon. It was scary." He snuggled his face back into her shoulder.

Jackie resumed rocking; the runners gave out a soft squeak. "The police came by earlier, but Blake sweet-talked them, convinced them there was nothing wrong. Even allowed them to search the house."

Monica scratched at her cheek. "Are you crazy? Why didn't you say something then, when they were here?"

"You've got to understand how scared I was. It was safest to go along with Blake." She rubbed her hand in circles on her son's back. "David, would you please tell me exactly how Will ended up with the gun?"

"Sure." David wiped his forehead with the back of his hand. "In the fight with Blake, it got knocked from my hand. He must have picked it up then."

Will wriggled on Jackie's lap and twisted his neck so he could see David. His face was streaked with dirt. "It went off all by itself."

"We're all so glad you didn't get hurt." Zoey said.

Jackie stopped rocking. "Blake, I don't understand." Her voice quivered and her face grew sad. "Why did you harm…kill your twin sister?"

He twisted his neck so he could see her. "I need you to understand." He screwed up his face as if feeling an unbearable pain. "I did it for you and me and Will. We belong together, Jackie. I'm sure you'll see that someday. Gwendolyn was cold, uncaring, like my mother must have been. She would have harmed Will. I didn't see it at first because I was so glad to be re-united with my twin."

"Did you take Will?"

"You see, I let myself in. That key. In the flower pot. It was so easy. You looked so beautiful sleeping there, like an angel. I closed Will's door and shook his shoulder to wake him. I told him about a trick, a game really, we were playing. Hide and seek. You'd try to find him, and in a few days we'd win and surprise you. After Will came with me that night, I wanted Gwendolyn to watch him for a few days. That was all I asked of her. I figured with a day care business, she'd know what to do." Blake swallowed. "You see, my plan was I'd find Will and be a hero. Your hero, Jackie." His eyes were pleading with her. "You liked the game we were playing, didn't you Will? A joke we were playing on your mama, right?"

Will wrapped his arms around his mother's neck.

"Gwendolyn took him camping in those woods, but people were looking for him, so she had to hightail it out of there. She brought him to that lousy motel.

"She had an idea that she could sell a fake DNA concoction to parents, bamboozle them into thinking their kids could be taller, or smarter, or some other nonsense. She said parents would pay a lot of money. Said our mother had sold babies and made lots of money. Sold me—me—the bitch!" His lips trembled.

Zoey and Monica exchanged looks.

"Then I saw Gwendolyn in Home Depot. Afterward, I put two and two together and realized she was the one who'd kidnapped that little girl. I didn't want to believe it. I knew then that she was out of control. Dangerous. I confronted her at her house. That poor little girl was locked in a bedroom, and Gwendolyn explained to me how she had abducted her. She was so matter of fact about it. She was going to take some of that child's blood for her DNA scheme. Said she was going to take some of Will's too. What else might she do? I had to stop her.

"She'd changed the rules on me. All she was supposed to do was take care of Will. I told her I was going to shut down her operation. Return the little girl to her parents. She went ballistic. Came at me with a pair of scissors. That's when I smashed her head with a vase. I didn't mean to kill her. I had to protect Will. You see that, don't you, Jackie?

"By then, I wasn't thinking straight. I took her body to Jake's garage, I don't know why. Then I went back to Gwendolyn's house and took care of that little girl. I put her own clothes back on and brought her to the day care center. A light was on inside, so I figured Joey was still there. Lots of times, he stayed late. I knew he would take care of her. There was a fence around the playground, so I thought she'd be safe in there.

"I didn't want any kids to be hurt. Jackie, tell me you understand. I need that, do you hear me Jackie?" He was crying and his face was twisted in despair.

Jackie looked away. "I don't know what to say." It was silent for a long time except for the creak of the rocker and the rain that had begun to pelt the windows. In the distance, Zoey heard police sirens; their whooping grew louder as they approached the house.

CHAPTER 43

The next week, Zoey sat in Principal Kroger's office and watched him enter data into his laptop. His curtains were drawn against the sun. She drummed her fingers on the arm of the chair. "You wanted to see me?"

He slammed the cover of the laptop shut as if it had just bitten him. "You ignored the meeting I asked you to have with me."

"I do apologize, but I did leave a message for you. I was in Pepperell researching information to find Will Ravinski." Zoey made sure her voice sounded humble, defeated even.

"Apparently you were successful. It was all over the local paper. "

"Yes."

He stood, walked to the front of his desk and leaned against it. "The Board met last night. After a great deal of discussion, we agreed to reinstate your pay. However, you will remain on leave." He handed her a piece of paper. "All the pay that was withheld, will be ..." He sniffed, and stopped. Zoey could see him working the muscles in his jaw as if he were chewing a bitter herb that, eventually, he would have to swallow. "All withheld pay will be issued to you in a check at the end of this week."

She took the paper from his desk, glanced at it, repressed a smile, and stood. "Why, thank you." Without another word, she left the office.

Kurt was interviewing a mystery writer in Boston, Judy Campbell, and Monica wanted to try a new restaurant that had opened near the waterfront, The Captain's Table. Zoey was to join them for lunch when her meeting was over.

When Zoey reached Boston, she called her sister on her cell phone. "Monica, you said this restaurant was off Seaport Boulevard. Is that right?"

"Yes. It becomes Northern Avenue. Then left on Jackson Street. Right on Ridge Way. You can't miss it. Has a blue and white awning." She cleared her throat. "By the way, how'd the meeting go with Mister-Stick-Up-His-Ass?"

Zoey laughed. "Okay. Tell you when I see you."

"By the way, David is here."

"No! Monica, you had no right—"

"See you soon." Monica clicked off.

Zoey thought about turning her car around and heading home, but decided it was best to go ahead. Besides, she was hungry. Upon entering the restaurant, she admired the expensive chrome décor, white table cloths, and waitresses in crisp blouses, black vests and slacks. Monica and Kurt waved from a window table with an ocean view. As she approached, David raised his eyebrows and grinned. Zoey believed he could light up all of Boston with that smile. A platter of appetizers was on the table. All three had glasses of wine, menus and small plates with portions of meat. Wine, a menu and an empty plate were waiting for Zoey.

After she filled them in about the meeting, Monica said, "This restaurant owner, Archibald Thatcher, has similar restaurants in New York City and Tampa. His family originally came from Boston. Since a number of relatives still call Beacon Hill home, he thought he'd give it a try right here." She pointed to a fried piece on the platter. "Wild boar belly." Then she identified the other items. "Alligator sausage, and that's reindeer rump, and rattlesnake with essence of bacon."

Leave it to Monica to find a place like this, just like her, flashy and attention grabbing. Zoey swallowed and gingerly took a piece of alligator sausage.

A waitress approached. Her gold-plated name tag read "Liz." Her eyes were prominent, her waist bulged and her legs were thick and muscular. "Ready to order?"

"What do you suggest?" asked Kurt.

"The barbecued python salad is popular, so is the elk chop." She blinked her eyes and licked her lips at the same time. "The chop is stuffed with duck. It comes with a Bordelaise sauce."

Everyone studied the menu. After they had ordered, Monica asked her sister, "How's Jackie doing?"

"She's strong and resilient, so is Will. And she and Guy have come to an arrangement.

"Oh?"

She laughed. "It's not what you're thinking. On weekends, she's agreed to let Will stay with Guy and his mother. They're thrilled. I doubt Jackie will ever get back with Guy, but they're on good enough terms, at least when it concerns their son."

After Liz served their meals, they chatted and ate slowly, savoring the unusual tastes. As they were finishing desert, whipped figs with confectionery sugar, Kurt said, "Todd will go to trial for selling drugs. Since it's not a first offense, he'll probably get put away for quite a few years."

"A nasty character." David put down his fork and wiped his mouth with his napkin. "That Butch Crow is another unsavory person, but he doesn't actually break the law."

"Well, Monica, we've got a few stories we need to write for the magazine."

Zoey directed her comment to David. "Comes close to crossing that line, though. He twists the rules quite a bit."

"True."

Monica cocked her head at her husband. "Well, love, we do have a magazine to get out." After the four of them settled the bill and left a generous tip, Kurt stood and his wife joined him. They said their goodbyes and, holding hands, left the restaurant.

David looked wistful as he and Zoey watched the couple leave. There was silence between them as they turned their attention to the ocean swells outside the window. He reached across the table and covered Zoey's hand with his. "I just want to be with you." He paused and drew in a deep breath. "What do you say?"

She withdrew her hand, sat back in the chair, and studied him. Looking down at the tablecloth, she said, "I...I don't think I'm ready yet."

She heard David sigh. "I can't wait forever."

Zoey felt tears forming as David stood, put down his napkin and slowly walked out of the restaurant. She sat alone and watched waves crest, and then break, as tears spilled down her cheeks.

Made in the USA
San Bernardino, CA
20 October 2018